NORMA

SARAH MINTZ

Invisible Publishing
Halifax | Fredericton | Picton

Library and Archives Canada Cataloguing in Publication
Title: Norma / Sarah Mintz.
Names: Mintz, Sarah, author.
Identifiers: Canadiana (print) 20230571034
             Canadiana (ebook) 20230571042
             ISBN 9781778430404 (softcover)
             ISBN 9781778430411 (EPUB)

Classification: LCC PS8626.I699 N67 2024 | DDC C813/.6—dc23

Edited by Melanie Simoes Santos
Cover design by Anonymous
Interior design by Megan Fildes | Typeset in Laurentian
With thanks to type designer Rod McDonald

Invisible Publishing is committed to protecting our natural environment. As part of our efforts, both the cover and interior of this book are printed on acid-free 100% post-consumer recycled fibres.

Printed and bound in Canada.

Invisible Publishing | Halifax, Fredericton, & Picton
www.invisiblepublishing.com

Published with the generous assistance of the Canada Council for the Arts, the Ontario Arts Council, and the Government of Canada.

   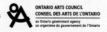

"Thus they gathered in a pell-mell of mad confusion and the earth groaned under the tramp of men as the people sought their place."

—*THE ILIAD*

THE OLDER I GET, THE DIRTIER I FEEL. I'm sixty-seven. I have short grey hair. My body is a murky site of mutant growth. I imagine dressing loudly in a sequin gown and metallic hat, catching the sun and corrupting an eye—if I was seen I wouldn't want to be seen. I don't think I was always like this. But now that it's here, this thought feels like the only thought I've ever had. One running thought, and I'm always in the middle of it. I used to feel busy. I used to be occupied. Always making dinner and folding laundry. Setting alarms and getting the day going. I used to iron. I used to read. I used to balance the books and answer the phones. And now it seems like one book is as good as any other book is as good as anything on TV is as good as anything on the radio—sometimes I think nothing is any good. Maybe I'm not looking hard enough. Maybe I'm looking too hard. Listen, I know I've become ridiculous. But, you know, rats, cats, fucking dogs—they just run around until their bodies are spent. Birds fly then fall into the ocean. So what's the use in feeling turned out by youth and betrayed by middle age?

***

Amelia Landover: I know you have Jason.

Derek DeMarco: There's nothing you can do about it, Amelia. If you tell anyone, they'll find out that I'm Jason's real father.

Amelia Landover: What do you want, Derek?

Derek DeMarco: You know what I want. Jason. He's mine. You're mine. I want us to be a family again.

Amelia Landover: You're delusional. We were never a family. I'll never leave Thurston for someone like you.

Derek DeMarco: I know you love me! Jason proves that our love is real! Leave with me or I'll tell Thurston everything!

A gang of Russian soap fans are relying on me. For the last three months, I've been typing out the lives and loves of the Landover and Callister families in two-minute increments for fifty cents a minute—or it's fifty cents if you can type fifty cents worth in a minute. If a minute takes six minutes because the speech is garbled or the recording is obscured by another recording of a deep-voiced Russian saying the things the characters are saying like it's one long emotionless speech, then fifty cents a minute is more like ten cents a minute—but fifty cents might as well be ten cents to me; I just like the soaps, or anyway, I'm trying to stay active.

Paradise Bluffs was a short-lived 1980s American soap opera with an enduring, primarily Eastern European fan base. The Russians found me—or I found them, or we found an amicably anonymous working relationship—through the monopolistic transcription site DERG, working slogan: *We'll sit screen-side for you, maybe we were going to anyway.*

I liked the soap fans so much I invaded their lives. Only a little, and they haven't noticed. I once posted on a Ted Kinder message board in praise of the young hunk's oiled body, re: the episode where Ted got caught in the rain with the new girl in town—the stunning, dark, and mysterious Andrea Wesley. The rain bounced off Ted, and he stood there glistening, gazing hotly at Andrea. "Swoon!" I said, and posted a picture of Ted, shirtless. No one replied to my comment. The conversation went on around me. Others noticed that the relationship between Thurston and Amelia in 1987 was peak Thurston and Amelia and made collage-like cut-outs of the love affair, sparkling in pixel hearts on dated websites. They couldn't believe how Amelia had ruined everything with her lies. How could she help it though? It could happen to anyone kidnapped as a child and raised on the something-that-stops-at-nothing of Vivienne La-Roque—Vivienne, whom Amelia's father, Phillip Callister, left for Amelia's mother, Juliana. Amelia was tragic, absolutely. There are hundreds of sites in Cyrillic script, in Latin script, devoted to the plot, the many plots, in detail microscopic, not an episode missing—not a character, a relationship, a hairstyle. I became lost for an hour if not a day if not a week on a website ranking the three-thousand-plus looks of Christie Callister—with minor attention paid to the costume design of Janice White and, later, David Gelding (not an insubstantial change).

Pristine Christie's following extended beyond her time on *The Bluffs*—which, while it enjoys unexpected niche legacy, didn't really *hit* in North America. Christie (Kaitlyn Durante) went on to star in the majors—ten years on *Love and Life* and twelve on *Rockcliff Falls*.

And while the conventions for current, ongoing soaps are worldwide events, with thousands lining up for Brock McAdams or Delaney Coombs, the universe of discontinued serials has its only real-world counterpart in basements on VHS tapes with hand-drawn labels. The online existence of a world that contains the best years of many an actor and many a housewife is as marginal as the discoloured sign of a dead grocery store cracking beneath the sign of a larger grocery store—awe at the immense amount of life that fills obscurity and seventh place.

My husband's father, Horace, for example, once owned a steel factory in Montreal. He inherited it from his father, dead, age fifty, colon cancer. Horace, when he was young and eager and keen, put up the frames of innumerable Montreal buildings. His bones, the bones of the city, forgotten under the weight of time before the internet. What could he be now, remembered forever in an online filing? A social media fan page for the steel industry? Forgotten under the weight of information after the internet. But if you turn off the power, but if you put out the sun, nothing gets its day. Obviously. That's what my husband would've said: "Obviously." Hank said that whenever I tried to make a point or sound smart. "Where d'you get this shit?" he'd say, smirking, shaking his head, chuckling, as if to an audience, as if saying, "Get a load of this one," pointing with his thumb and waiting for laughter to come and go. And it's not that I'm happy he's dead, it's just that I don't know why I don't feel worse. Maybe I do. Maybe it's grief that causes me to sit in front of the computer day after day, transcribing off-air American soap operas.

Not only soaps—I misspoke. There's a wealth of worlds from which I write out my time and fill out their fetishes. Soap operas, writing retreats, painters' podcasts, political talk shows, and more and more and so much incest. The incest sticks with you. Gets inside, if you can understand that. You listen with guilty fascination, hunting out any other files that colour in the affair, the incident. And when the files play and you type absently, you're in the room. The same room as Detective Amber Goodwin on February 20

"...with Inspector Mcreally and Doug Deleanor. Doug, can you state your name and date of birth."

Doug Deleanor:	Douglas Rhodes Deleanor. July 6, 1985.
Amber Goodwin:	And can you tell me what happened on November 19 of last year.
Doug Deleanor:	What happened... what happened was that, like, just like before, like the other time we talked about.
Amber Goodwin:	Your daughter, Marigold, was sitting on the couch. And how did it get started? I mean, what exactly did you do?
Doug Deleanor:	What I did, I don't know what I did. I just... I was rubbing her shoulders, I think.
Amber Goodwin:	You were rubbing her shoulders. Can you... And then... How did that progress? Or did it progress?
Doug Deleanor:	What... It was... I was sitting next to Mari, she was wearing a skirt, and I think it was just... I had my arm around her, sort of like rubbing her shoulders. Probably...maybe...moved my arm down and put my hand on her leg.
Amber Goodwin:	Okay. Okay, is that all that happened? You just rubbed her shoulders and put your hand on her leg?

Doug Deleanor: Well, it was like... How it happened, I did put my hand between her legs, I mean. I think after that, I got down...I put my mouth...

Amber Goodwin: Where did you put your mouth?

Doug Deleanor: I mean, I pulled her skirt up, I put my mouth, like...on her thigh, like...and then I think that was it.

Amber Goodwin: Okay. On her thigh. Okay. And was that the only time?

Doug Deleanor: There was the time at the house on Broadland, in the bedroom. I think I mentioned it. It was... I don't know. I don't know. It was maybe the first time. She just wanted to hug me, she's just like that, it isn't her fault. I don't know. It made me uncomfortable, when she was just being, like, a normal kid, because it would make me... I felt things.

Amber Goodwin: When she would hug you, you were uncomfortable because you felt things?

Doug Deleanor: Right, right. Not always. I mean, when she was younger I never thought anything like that. It was just in the past few years. When she started getting her period, I guess. I don't know what happened. Like, she started hugging me and I'd...I'd just have those feelings. And sort of rub her shoulders or whatever else...

There's guilt over feeling frigid at the loss of your life partner after forty-seven years, noting relief—*relief*—or just nothing—not able to note anything. Then there's guilt over finding intrigue in the real-life incestuous deposition of a man who has no choice but to trust the police with his private information in a world of outsourcing and flimsy NDAs. And there's guilt over being moved to lust, then action, then tears over the bud of a girl who dares to wear a skirt around the house. I mean Doug—Doug was torn apart.

The transcriptions, the problem with the transcriptions, is that they contain nothing of the tender voice of Amber Goodwin, a voice you might, when flat from a printout, assign harsh, or not harsh enough, judgment upon—such judgment extending obviously to the overloaded voice of Doug. Doug who skirts the meat of it, Doug whose voice slows then breaks, speeds then stops. Doug who wept because he knew he must weep. What if we lived in a world in which no one jerked around at that which occurred—would Doug still be sad? I don't know. I doubt it. Unless he was sad about something else.

It isn't all sensational. The sensation isn't always sordid. The sensation doesn't always make you wonder about your own morality and your own humanity and the humanity of others—what seems like most others—living public lives at, say, the grocery store, and private lives on couches with their daughters, or private lives in the lives of others, or private lives in the lives of fictional others. Most of the audio files available for transcription are jargon, compu-jargon, business nonsense—material around which an uninitiated person may find it impossible to wrap their head, and, as such, wrangle: "So you would wanna, if that's your plan, you'd wanna architect it as such that you have a toggle that is, you know, a toggle that is solid that we can make sure is turned off in the weRAMP environment and turns off in the server, service itself. Um, now assuming you've done that— End of message." The contextless mass. The worlds of which you will never be a part, of which you don't wish to be a part, but immerse yourself in nonetheless for a moment or too many moments, enough moments that you feel you're in the world and you've chosen not to understand. You struggle to escape the impossible multi-cult of various meanings.

Detached, then, from the worlds made within the world as it appears, you join or watch or sit or watch. You are listening: "What are you reading in the bread that suggests to you that it's fresh?" The line makes you laugh in your kitchen, and the laugh alone you find pure and sincere and lost on empty space. A woman in a grocery store with a subject, presumably. The two of them discussing the supermarket. Discussing the bread and imparting to the items strange significance. You assume the task is taken up for marketing purposes, but the interrogation has a psychiatric tone. "What are you reading in the bread that suggests to you that it's fresh?" the interviewer asks. Although she doesn't ask. That isn't the real line. Few of these are the real lines. The real line would be something like "And, um, what do you think... How... What is it that you read or see...Um, what are you reading in the bread that suggests to you about it...about that, uh, that it's fresh?" But you don't write that unless the transcription *requestee* has *requested* a *verbatim*, and, so, virtually unreadable, transcript.

So DERG makes readable the way fast food makes edible an input of real messy bits polished into, processed into, itself—working slogan revised: *Taste of DERG*. Done, like, with lab-made spice, branded, trademarked, sprinkled into everything—that is: readable by the inconsistent application of company-specific grammar.

In the style guide, they advise against informal contractions. In the style guide, they advise that when one can cut a comma, one should cut a comma. There are no semicolons allowed. No colons, no parentheses, no em dash. In the style guide, they advise not to change the structure of the speech. In the style guide, they advise not to change the meaning of the speech. When the meaning is unclear, when the meaning is elusive, how does one—I, me—determine which words are superfluous?

"*Shhheeeeeeeeeeeee*, Norma, what're ya on about?"

Listen, Hank, if you're gonna be dead, be dead. This is a real conversation, a real conversation with a dead man, and I know it's only partial—I know the meaning isn't hard—but the meaning *feels* real, like real conversations generating the kind of off-the-cuff grammar that just emerges—not grammar presumed to exist, that shiny magazine grammar made from studies where they cut tails and make rules from the mean, or else those studies with hyper tail focus for when the mean is too messy. Stick to the style guide. Nobody makes any sense. Everything is context and flailing limbs. Here, the context was the grocery store, limbs dislocated. All you have to go on is a suspicion of bread.

Subject in a supermarket with a woman with a tape recorder or perhaps with her phone set to record, or with a system that saves and holds this moment and any other moment you ask it to forever, or until you throw it away. But still, they say once it's made, it's made. But if no one listens, I'm not sure it continues to be. "It's not a lot of variety, but when you need a cake, you need a cake, right?" the interviewee says in regard to a limited selection of baked sweets, and somehow it strikes you as both wrong and profound. Or correct, though accidently or naively borne out by some diurnal profundity.

The interviewer asks the woman to be taken to the freshest item in the bakery, like it's a test. It's unclear whether the interviewer knows the answer. The interviewee walks over, shuffles, and there's a man's voice in the distance squawking over a phone call in the produce department. The shuffling woman answers that the freshest thing in the bakery is "probably the baked breads." The interviewer asks, "And why do you think these are the freshest things in the bakery?" seeking meaning, making static. The interviewer goes on: "What are you seeing or reading in them that suggests that to you?"

You're giddy.

I'm giddy.

At home, in my pyjamas, in a room filled with waxed wrappers and plastic bags with yellow smiling faces, I'm tickled by the idea of reading bread. I laugh; I look around. There's nothing to do with it; it rests, settling in the space between the discrete pieces of filth all over my floor.

"And I know you said because you saw someone bring it out into the bakery, but is there anything else, any other cues that suggest to you that these are the freshest items here?" The interviewer is strange and stiff. "Is this as fresh as this or this? How do you know which item is fresher than one or the other? Do these items that you've identified as being less fresh get credit for freshness because they're in the same section?" Who gets credit for freshness.

The audio file ends with the interviewer in the car, listening to rush-hour rock radio, the swishing of the fabric of her jacket cutting at my eardrums through noise-cancelling headphones. She mutters, "Oh my God," and the file ends. A brief relation. Me with them. Following them around the grocery store, bedroom sociologist listening to no end little marketeers work over a field of well-stocked bread stores— I hope, I dream, that someone eats the cake.

***

The grocery store I like altogether. I mean, I like the grocery store. I like all the grocery stores. There are three within twelve blocks of my house, and I visit them all. I don't always buy things; I just like to walk around. I walk to the grocery store; I walk around the grocery store. On the walk there, black-edged snow melts slow into holey puckers showing all the wet ends of things. I see, for example, the flattened carcass of a sea bird in the gutter between the street and the sidewalk. Although on second look, it's only a length of tree bark. On the same walk, for example, I see the root system of a tree emerged from the concrete like the distended intestines of an aged thing, and then, when I look again, note that it's only a gummy black T-shirt twisted into a small pile. This is the same day I spot a comically steamrolled snake in the centre of a crosswalk—but then, it's only a flecked green bungee cord fallen off the back of a truck. Not long after, I come across two immense hamsters sitting on either side of an asphalt driveway. Though it seems that the final appearance is just an ill-defined wish for large guard hamsters to take the place of dead yellow grass in weathered planters the city over.

Making the reward manifest: an apophenic arranging of information leading to the seeking out and finding of more such information. In conjunction with *what*—I'm building the synchronous. For example. I can filter files for accent. I can filter files for subject matter. I can filter files for audio quality. I can cross-check names of transcription agencies that act as incoming depositories for a whole host of organizations against affiliates associated with or listed by larger, heavier, thicker, more substantial entities and institutions. Some orgs go direct; others use middlemen upon middlemen. There are two middlemen in my county, which I found by way of search and the strange junction between the data-fed helpers promising products and the black-box workings of the thing that sees and knows and offers through bought-and-sold sponsors: Skontac and Verve. Employees of which are then searchable through other orgs, and then, when primed to see a Kim, Ujang, or Harvinder, I scan the files of a particular quality within a particular subject within a particular accent category, and it's only one month or two months or three months since your husband died, when you might come upon your very own hometown. The Stockton Institution, for example, uses Stockton's own Skontac Word Assist Ltd., who outsource to DERG and enter the worldwide one-of-us, so I added local outsourcers Kim Manny, Ujang Feeling, and Mick Crawly to my favourites on the DERG interface. Click on the Kim Manny file and be subjected to mostly low-quality output with skewed high-quality ratings due to introductory robots upsetting the assessment system. Though sometimes I go among the prisoners to hear them bitch out their sleeping girlfriends anyway.

Robot: Hello. You have a collect call from...

Flav: Flav.

Robot: ...at the Stockton Institution Stockton District Stockton County. Be aware. This call is being recorded. This call is subject to third-party review.

Any attempt to add a third party to any call will result in inmate disciplinary action, and the involved end user's phone number will be globally blocked. To learn more about the InGuardian calling cards, please visit www.InGuardian.com, select Institutional Security, Telephone Access, Calling Cards. To accept the charges for this call, press one. To refuse this call, hang up.

Flav: Hello?

Heshy: [inaudible]

Flav: Hello?

Heshy: I said, what you want?

Flav: I am calling you.

Heshy: [inaudible]

Flav: What you saying?

Heshy: I am sleeping.

Flav: Wake your ass up.

Heshy: [inaudible]

Flav: Wake your ass up! Heshy! Wake the fuck up out of bed!

Heshy: Don't say my name on here.

Flav: I say what I want. You're going to wake your ass up, get that big ass out of bed, shake them fat titties into the phone like [inaudible].

Heshy: Shut up.

Flav: Why are you going to say that? I am calling you.

Heshy: I'm sleeping.

Flav: Wake the fuck up! You know you wouldn't be like this if I was with you, so why you doing this to me now?

Heshy: What you saying?

Flav: I am calling you.

Heshy: I know that.

Flav: I want you to get your fucking ass up and tell me some shit. Roll them tig ass bitties over.

Heshy: Shut up.

Flav: Shut your ass up.

Robot: This call will be terminated in four minutes.

Heshy: Call me a different time.

Flav: I call you when I fucking call you! I'm in jail, don't you know I'm in jail? I don't just come out when I want.

Heshy: I'm fixing to hang up the phone.

Flav: What are you saying?

Heshy: You can't just expect me to do whatever you say.

Flav: I can very well. I fucking love you, Heshy.

Heshy: I love you too. Call me a different time.

Robot: The caller has hung up.

Versus the Verve files—employees favourited: Melody Carmina, Harvinder Gill, Raj Reddy, Cybil Billet, Franz Kippel—in the earned & gifted-local, which are largely dull: school boards, advisory councils, corporate arms, interviewers, interviewees, prospects, marks, focus groups. Nothing is less interesting than six people with a shared vocabulary in nothing. But I'm like the police-scanner people—learning how to listen without any application for the knowing. Tell a buddy. About this thing. Search-engine people. I'm getting good at it. Skontac and Verve. The voices but not the faces of Flav and Heshy. Their rough love—is it love?

Ask DERG forum user Katieyy21, who, after having picked up the first drop of the Kim Manny Flav files, checks what she knows against the Stockton Institution's prisoner database and posts:

FROM THE COUNTY'S PRISON RECORDS:

> **S42665:** Fulstad "Flav" Johnstone
> **DOB:** 4/26/1988
> **TATTOOS:**
>   **BACK:** two flaming bags of money
>   **RIGHT UPPER ARM:** "JJ" above a woman's face;
>   **LEFT CALF:** a pair of dice each showing the number six
>   banner between the dice reading "Let it Ride"

This must be him, you guys.

Forum member feline replies:

feline | That's him for sure. I had a 2015 file where Flav's *then*-gf Dell was telling him that *Fulstad Junior* was gonna be a Johnstone, and Flav said the kid couldn't have the Johnstone name because Dell cheated on him. He was emotional, crying that it was his dad's name. Actually from the file: "No bitch snakes Stone, you hear?" LOL.

L.Oena2222 | Ohhhh, I had a DUI bodycam with Flav AND Dell! Must have been after 2015, because they had TWO kids in the car and Dell was SCREAMING, "Shut up lil Flav, Shut up lil!" while the kid was crying. He must have been at least four years old.

S_illa | omg, I wonder if lil Flav was a Johnstone ;)

KarkarMcleod | I had a file where Dell was running his "dogfood business" for him while he was locked up. But I think by then they'd broken up. They were all business, and Flav even asked about Heshy!

LittleLish | Guys, Heshy is Dell's little sister! I wrote out a three-way call with all of them. I don't know how he dumped Dell and knocked up Heshy, but they were talking about bringing their kids to school together, then Flav told Heshy he loved her, but he had to talk to "Big Momma" about some business.

feline | Holy shit.

KarkarMcleod | Damn.

Katiey21 | You guys, I can't wait till Flav Season Three drops.

Open-throated cybersleuths. Beyond intrigue, more personal than the police-scanner man—I'm no ham scanner with an interest in radios. Not just listening, just hearing—hungry. The female slink of the online underbelly, or upper belly, soft and creeping, intrigue that stays home—the part of the belly that lies flabby forward.

"What could go wrong?" someone thought or didn't think; the accumulation of wrongs righted by soft-hearted mothers announcing "never again" haven't yet had an impact on future files and the unseen hazards made real by widows with nothing but time. So I get to know what I know and align my mind to that multi and make synchronicity out of the fed-and-sped intuition of the internet—fleshed out and operating as a monstrously deformed *anima mundi*. Deformed by what? Maybe deformity is only a mistake of variability, and this deformed machine, seeping eyeball of a world spirit, is one of many, and for all its life and vitality, it never gets to be as beautiful as the most beautiful version. Because nature tries and fails to no end? To see what fits. And what doesn't fit can only be discarded; and what doesn't fit can't just fit because it hurts not to fit. Sorry, little spirit—sorry, little spark—not everyone wins. *Naturam expellas furca, tamen usque recurret.*

"*Shuuuuddup…*" Hank would say or sing—twinkling when he said it? Or was he just a hassling old man hassling again? "Who cares?" he'd come back with if he knew my thoughts ran like this or if he does now from where he rests. "Enough."

***

Inside the grocery store, everything is tidy and colourful. Sometimes there are sales, and I like to imagine the money

I could save if I was in the market for a bag of mixed sea-food or a trio of hot sauces. The store nearest my house, the Savery, is where, if I had to pick a point, I'd point there, and more to the point, as the moment I met Marigold.

I'm familiar with the Ujang Feeling files. A Skontac worker, he mainly submits police recordings, and having "favourited" Feeling and being a preferred user for the time I've devoted to the DERG org, I get early pick of the files. They come up neat in rows and columns, arranged by preferences: favourited users, sorted further by accent, sub-ject matter, quality, length of file, and number of speakers. The Feeling files are somewhat rare, or else there are users more preferred than me, with even more time to stare at the screen—watching at night, perhaps, during breakfast, lunch, dinner, mid-afternoon snacks, late-night snacks—sitting at their computers, filling the keyboards with crumbs, making the screens sticky with soda—maybe those users more extreme than me snatch them up, those highly prized Feeling files. Most of the Verve files are so common and terrible as to go unclaimed for hours, whereas the Skontac files, the majority of which are submitted by Ujang Feeling, move quickly for all their sordidness and quality recording.

Could be a common curiosity among preferred transcrib-ers to find intrigue in various states of the carceral system, as found in the Feeling files. We're getting statements. We're hearing the story. Though the time a pregnant Hoa told the cop that Dinh was trying to get her to abort her baby and she'd spent the evening in a hotel with Dinh texting his wife and exposing the lies, only for Dinh to empty her purse, steal her car, and brandish a gun at the concierge for no reason anyone could determine—that's the time I thought, *Why? What do I need with these Skontac Feeling files? Maniacs dump-*

ing their belongings on the street. Is that who I want to be? Not me. And since I must entertain every encounter as though it's me living each scene—in the parking lot, in the hotel with Dinh, on the phone with Dinh's wife—I feel no urgency toward the Feeling files. Though I claim them often, out of some hometown possessiveness, I suppose. Or because I feel knowing and skilled and blessed to come upon the gift of local gossip. And the Dinh file was easy enough, but the content was repetitive even for its sensation. Cheap and fusty. Dirt under the nails, lint and hair stuck to the pant leg. While the sleeping Heshy managed charm like magic.

But the Feeling file that's led me to linger in a familiar grocery store, use each checkout one at a time, meet each cashier, hover over meats, sniff the fish, eyeball the plastic hats, finger the flowers, ask questions about dirt quality, and nurture a new interest in breads, in cakes—is a gift. From me to me. This reward being even greater than that of finding a quality file from Verve's Harvinder—though each reward offers jolts of movement, motion, removed from whatever process one assumes made way for the jolt itself. What lizard lobster chimp would puzzle over me with this new prize, when I seek out the Deleanor family online and find that those with profiles keep high privacies, but one of them has been tagged in a photo of a company softball team at the Savery's employee picnic.

***

She isn't a real cashier, I suppose; she just stands by the self-checkout counters in case anyone needs help. Or in case someone is trying to steal. I assume. Actually, I don't know if her role is to prevent theft or really why she stands there, as I tend to think her twinkling blue-violet eyes would offer more encouragement than discouragement to would-be thieves.

The girl stands, leans, on the side of an employee podium. Doris, known only by her name tag, approaches: "How are ya, hon?" The young girl's arms are crossed over her chest, over her name tag, but she's what I expected, what I would've expected had I known how to say I expected it when I found the fuzzy picture online. She's slight and delicate, with wispy blond hair and painfully thin translucent skin. She sighs, "It's just a lot. Dealing with this." Doris purses her lips sympathetically.

Before the Deleanor file and the softball search, I wouldn't have thought to sit around the grocery store. I like to walk there, walk around, look at the deals, and emerge refreshed, or at least emerge. Leave, I mean. I like to walk around, and then I like to leave and then sometimes visit another grocery store and make a day of finding deals and maybe or maybe not buying deals. But I'm caught up in something now; I have to follow through on coincidence made meaningful by ads recommending Skontac after having found Verve when searching for local deposits of obscure information, like a police scanner man wearing a sweaty mesh baseball hat in a shack in his mother's backyard, but me, with my hunched shoulders in a taffy-coloured kitchen in my dead husband's house.

Is this why the young girl shifting her weight back and forth, leaning on the podium, standing up straight, folding her arms, dropping her arms, turning, swaying amidst six self-checkout counters has become interesting? Or has she always been interesting? I've seen her before; I'm sure I have. I imagine now how my thoughts were then, when I must've seen her, and how she was then, before I knew anything about her, when I'd just come to buy groceries to eat groceries like normal. I think she was always interesting because she was young and pretty and had this way or witchery that sometimes certain young people have, capturing, inadvertently, an essential art—art by accident? They just get to be beautiful nature for a day or for a month or for a year or ten—it doesn't last. It's always temporary—youth is beauty, youth as beauty—though what could I know about charm and beauty, nature and art?

So I don't want the girl; I don't want to pursue her, or have her, or do what people do with beauty, whyever it exists as a girl who works in a grocery store. For breeding, for babies—how do you say it? How do you make sense of beauty? God-given, nature-given, you can only make it ugly. Use it up. I'm not beautiful. And I'm not a breeder. Hank and I never had children. It wasn't discussed, we didn't bother, it never occurred. Besides, there wasn't much to us in bed. Body like a dull slab. I did the dishes, I did the laundry, et cetera. Whatever should have come of it didn't come of it. So nothing of it. Anyhow, I don't care one way or another about the girl's beauty, other than to note that it's there. That's the strange thing. It's just there, and you can have ideas about it, but you can't really explain it.

So I'm LOOKING at the girl. LOOKING at the girl. Youth. No blisters, no bruises, no errant hairs, warts, veins, vessels, flaps—not pieced together, poured whole. LOOKING like something makes sense. In spite of godless happenstance, a flower blooms to shame the weeds. But so, one plant's as good as another, in the right system, in a botanist's garden—but no. Stop pretending. In a forest full of orchids, animals step softly; in a bramble of Scotch broom, thrash and burn. Don't pretend. Stop pretending. It hurts, it aches, it's not for you, it's not for anybody—just an animal whose accident mimics hope, promises purity, transcends.

Everyone looks at her; everyone talks to her. She smiles demurely and bows her head, a little embarrassed. I know I know her. I know I've seen her. Coming across her father's Feeling file and the tagged shot at a company picnic—it isn't *nothing* fueling that. Doris just offers an *in*, and I take a seat. The small section beside the self-checkout counters is where a person sits with a coffee or with their heat-lamp-warmed chicken or a plastic tray of day-old sushi. And while I sit with a foam cup full of decent coffee—not bad anyway, tastes fine to me—listening to Doris talk to a familiar forlorn girl who has dropped her arms and angled her body in a way that I can see the tag on her chest, I am beyond convinced; I know it for sure: I've found the girl from the file, the girl from the internet.

***

I walk home from the grocery store beneath everything I've typed and seen and heard—everything added up. Doris and Marigold, in hushed tones, helping each other, holding each other, being there for one another. I'm not sure how they couldn't feel me, my delight. I was with them; though I sat to the side at the laminate table with a plastic seat held in place by a green metal bar, I sat listening, crouched over my coffee. I heard support, not much more than that, but I'm sure I've found her because I know I've seen her before—though not really, just like a background anybody maybe with a little of that lingering fascination of youth. Or do I just think that now? Having found her, I can't say whether I remember really seeing her before or if my mind is making more than there was to begin with. What can I say about the coincidence I cause? Just because I heard her father, and because I saw her at a distance, in a faraway way, wearing a hat on a hot day at a company picnic after having sought her—that doesn't mean some of it wasn't given from *without*—but where is *without* online, where *without* comes connected, where *without* digs out buried architecture with collective effort, making unmistakable an alignment between the inexplicable and the programmed? The meaningful alliance of things that I wouldn't have known to look for until they became meaningful to me cannot be undermined by whether or not I have any business looking for them in the first place and making that meaning mine, can they?

***

In my kitchen, across the crowded floor, I wade over to my computer and search my files. It's a Feeling file. I know that. Anyway, my already-transcribed files are all available and sorted by date—or I can sort them by money earned, or by grade received—but I'm a preferred user as determined by time in and awards issued—awards of almost entirely five stars out of five stars by the bots and men of DERG itself. No easy feat, as evidenced by the brutal reviews served up against DERG on worker forums. But I don't complain. I don't take a low score. I'm careful. I'm good at this. Any time a grader assumes they've heard something that is or isn't there and attempts to tarnish my near-perfect score, I have a defence. You will be docked one point for the grave error of not recording a name in the speaker section if there's reason to assume the name has been given. But certainly we can't assume the second speaker is referring to the third when they say, "Richard thought..."! Richard could be anywhere. Richard could be anyone. You don't expect me to make such an assumption, I might reply to the grader, who is now flagged by me and hopefully considered a more suspect grader all for the crime of questioning my judgment.

But I know it's been a few weeks anyway since I saw a Feeling file, so I scan the column by date, then sub-sort by favourite users and find Doug pretty quick.

"Just like before, like the other time we talked about," he tells Amber Goodwin.

The other time. I haven't heard about the other time. I didn't type out that file. There are no Doug sleuths on the forums. But the other files will come to me. It's devotion and coincidence and the new emerging universe that's led me to Doug's file; it must be, because of how things have arranged themselves, and it will be, because I can just turn on notifications and have the data sent direct. My interest has been growing; things are slowly getting clear. As I seek the details and they're filled out for me, Doug's story becomes more than all the other stories—beyond Flav, Heshy, Hoa, and Dinh. I've heard such stories before. But I think it must be there, the knowing I have about life at the grocery store. It's my town, my neighbourhood, and she's someone I've seen probably, one supposes, or reflects. I do go to the grocery store often. I mean, I go to all of them, but the Savery is only three blocks away.

And so seeking him out and then the girl afterward, it isn't so strange, it's only what's meant to be, what I've made it be. I've often looked up subjects and victims and villains and participants—it doesn't take long for information to gather together, to seek itself out. I've heard couples fighting for fourteen minutes over nothing that either one can pinpoint but amounts to something like neither listening while the other one screams. And I've seen their faces smiling in pictures together, tagging each other, hugging each other over piña coladas at Club Med all-inclusives.

So this isn't strange. That I know the girl, that I knew the girl, that I've uncovered more and more and can confirm that this is it: her father confessing to what I've heard is common, at least within my limited view of common, but is really an impossibly dense *unthinkable* common, crossing boundary after boundary of social, cultural, biological transgression, only to exist as a low version of myth.

And beyond possibly seeing her or knowing her prior (sure I did) was the familiarity, cool ease, and comfort in *his* voice. Is this a real villain? And what does my relationship with the wicked say about any assessment I might make about those who wander wet streets made wet for how wet looks on film? This is it: you don't know anything. Or, at least, I don't.

***

So I'm glued to it. I sit around the kitchen table refreshing the files. NEW I hit, NEW I hit, NEW. I could wait for the email notification that my favourite, most favourite, user has submitted another file, but what if someone claims the file in the twenty seconds it takes me to click the link? WHAT IF I'M IN THE BATHROOM? NEW I hit, NEW I hit, NEW. How long does it take? Well, it takes dedication, but I'm devoted to the story. The luridness of the whole thing suggests some alternative—hidden meaning, hidden depth—as if there are realities beneath realities.

Like, I remember—or made this memory of things thought afterwards, but it's shaped like a memory, although it's me in it, I see me, not my POV, but staged, the star—a small girl, maybe four or five years old. She's in a crowded place being dragged along by her mother—her prim, always moving, upright mother. She hears the phrase, as though a moment out of time, a predictable puzzle uttered: "the meaning of life." Maybe it was news discussed, a conversation in passing. Unknown. The phrase was isolated. The girl I see and have always thought was me thinks, *How stupid*, because she knows the meaning. She doesn't know the words that make the meaning, and she doesn't need to know. She doesn't try to find them. The meaning is so apparent that to ask the question is an insult to that which is fundamental. But how she knew without words what I haven't known since remains a mystery sought in sensation. Cheap realities masquerading as infinite complexities through a series of well-placed thrills.

If I can just know Marigold's mother, sister, brother, aunt, uncle, grandmother, dog, Marigold herself—I can figure it out. Who she is and why she suffers.

And what do I want with information void of meaning simulating meaning? Well, it isn't my fault if I have access. I'm the hired help. And how can the help not be interested in the lives of their betters? Like a butler gossiping to the maid, and I'm also the maid. What else do we have to talk about? We live here; don't get mad when *you* become the topic of conversation. What should we discuss instead? Philosophy? We're unrigorous, uninterested. Is Doris interested? Isn't the only thing that brought Doris and Marigold together a formal interview process? So I could comfort Marigold too. Not that I want to. It isn't that I want anything, not really. It's that I *know*. I know, and I have to keep knowing because otherwise the knowing doesn't mean anything. And if I can keep knowing and if I can help, maybe something would something something. Click. Shuffle. Falling dominoes.

***

I only started transcribing after Hank died so I could keep busy. Which is really absurd because I always resented how busy he kept me. He always needed something done or some attention paid. I even retired not long after he retired because he kept calling the office, because he couldn't keep himself to himself. They didn't care if he called. I was mostly by myself at the Park Lodge anyway, sitting out there in a tin annex off the business side of a middling golf course, hardly working for all the personal calls.

"It's where you left it, Hank... How should I know where you left your bucket hat?... No, no, I am not always moving everything... No, I haven't...I have not touched your fishing gear—it's in the garage! My God, Hank, I'll find it when I get home... It's a half day today... Well, because I want it to be, because I'm coming home at one o'clock... Listen, don't worry about it. No, it's fine. I'll find it this afternoon... Of course, yep, I'll pick up chicken... Your sister wants chicken anyway... Oh, she comes almost every night, Hank, why wouldn't I talk to her about what's for dinner?... Don't be ridiculous... Don't be ridiculous... Yeah, the rotisserie kind... Yeah, I like that one best too."

I took care of him. He was older than me but demanding, dependent. I ran errands with him and for him. I cooked for him; I laid out clothes for him—he was precise about his pants, not that he did much in a pair of fresh-pressed slacks, but he had a way he liked them. And though we didn't have kids, we had his mother and his sister Margery, and just like him, they were always needing and calling and expecting, or at least being. I always felt so put upon, always so at the whim of. And when Hank's mother died, somehow it got worse. I was needed more. I had to make the funeral arrangements, I had to call her friends, I had to handle the estate. And Hank in neat creases always seemed to be necessarily doing what he was doing, but what he was doing, I couldn't say; I was too busy doing.

Margery's death was a real blow. Hank was born eight minutes after Margery, and he'd never been without her. They were close without being close—the connection unstated, unexplored, constant. They'd never bothered to live their lives without each other, and they'd never done much of consequence with those lives. But they lived 'em.

Margery was an immense woman, and though her obesity would've implied something untoward about her health, instead it gave her an air of strength and unflappability. She was loud and blubbering and interesting and social, but unorganized—expectant that things should be done. Like her brother, my Hank, but he was without those red cheeks strained from laughing. He was the worst of all: quiet, disorderly, insistent on some organization that he found impossible to create outside of ordering it into place. The twins had chaotic minds—normal but ill-defined; their ideas weren't ideas but moments that came and went. Things that needed to be done were only orders given like whims that persisted through whining. Squeaky wheels, maybe.

But Margery gave me something beyond work, and her death seven months prior to Hank's was much more painful than when Hank's mother went the year before—it's been like a run of death, something I willed but never wanted. And so I get, for my unnamed desire, to drift, or else to suffocate—is that the feeling of total freedom? Is that something anyone really wants? Margery had given us a life; she was our link. In movement, on the sidewalks around town, she attracted attention and good spirits, and we got to ride alongside her. If I was sitting behind her taking notes and paying rent, it seemed like services well rendered for what she gave us in return: a presence in our small-but-not-small-enough-that-anyone-would've-known-us-otherwise   town. Margery's death was a weight on me I really couldn't lift. And I couldn't part the seas at the flea market, craft fair, or city council meeting to let Hank come and sit down and make him feel like he was meant to be anywhere. She'd always done that. So there was something about his heart and head and hands that began to pull on me with ever-increasing need after the death of his mother and then his Margery.

I found myself willing his demise, evilly, cruelly, with true malice and squinting eyes when he'd call on me to grab him something—to find him something for an ache, a pain—or to otherwise listen to his idea about some stupid thing he'd seen on TV or read about in the paper. So much of *us* had been buffered by *them* or *that*—his close family, our long jobs, a dailiness that had slipped, slipped, slipped and fell, fell and died.

His funeral in January was a bleak affair. We'd stopped knowing so many people. And the people we did know all thought that someone who knew us better was the right person to come and make speeches for my fat old man. Few came. I found myself eating triangles of tuna in the midst of a man Hank had fished with three times and who eyeballed the casket like it owed him something.

***

When Hank's mother, Penny, died, I cleared out her belongings. Most of her personal effects had been scrapped and swapped for the rented furniture that came with the room she'd been in for the past ten years. But I was responsible, at the time of her death, for organizing her affairs and disposing of anything she'd left behind that didn't belong to the home. The twins were too distraught to help, I was told, but Margery assured me, "There's hardly anything to be done."

On my own, the Sunday after Penny's funeral, in a dusty, sunny, cramped little room, I filled a garbage bag full of Penny's clothes for the Give 'n' Save. I filled a garbage bag full of pills, bathroom effects, twenty shades of maroon lipstick, perfume samples, a dirty bath mat, and a fluffy toilet seat cover for the dump. Then a box of pictures and a wicker sun hat from Acapulco for our basement, and a smaller box full of pearls and gold, crystals and plastic earrings for Margery. I knew she'd want the shiny things.

I took my time cleaning out the room. I'd loved Penny. She was a strange old woman—not by old-woman standards, as she was probably average, but by my own made-up standards that I apply willy-nilly to people I know and people I meet. She was open about everything, a babbling brook of thoughts and feelings, moods, aches, rages, memories, desires. She was always telling us how glad she was that we were all together, how happy she was to be with us. But along with profusely loving statements, nostalgic remembrances, idle musings, and complaints, she was incapable of listening to anyone. In answer to question or conversation, she'd go off on her own unrelated and utterly confusing tangent, often inspired by a fictional storyline, fantasy vacation, or ongoing bingo scandal. If she caught you on your own, in a hallway or outside the washroom, and she was in the mood for it, she'd give you an earful about the bingo caller's speed, the bingo caller's girlfriend, and the questionable circumstance in which this trashy girl, "not to gossip," won the biggest jackpot in Stockton County East Side Community Hall history. All the same, I was fond of her and her white hair and purple lipstick, her polyester pants and knit sweaters. And so, when I found a letter on a notepad in the drawer of the small black desk allotted to old Mother Penny by the Precious Memories Assisted Living Facility, I sat on the side of her naked mattress and read it twice.

Dear Camilla,

I'm sick to my stomach about the episode that aired on Friday, December 1, 2017. First of all, you're too old for this. Move on. Ron Black doesn't love you, and I don't think he ever did. He tolerated you, Camilla, and you drove him away. Now, I understand what it's like to be alone, let me tell you! My dear husband Horace died 34 years ago, and I've never remarried! I've never even looked at another man! You need to be more self-sufficient, Camilla, like me. I go to bingo, I take trips with the girls, Helena, Wanda, Dorothy, the whole gang. And I see my kids just about every day, my Hank and Margery! I never take them for granted, Camilla, and that's the key. Make your kids some oatmeal cookies, for God's sake. I don't know how old you are, but I'd guess in your fifties, and you can't be chasing men at that age. It's an absolute sin! As someone who has always rooted for you, Camilla, it's an embarrassment. All that to say, my dear, you've really gone too far this time. You can't trick Ron Black into sleeping with you, Camilla! And even if the fertility drugs help you get pregnant, what about the poor child that comes of it? What are you thinking? This comes from a friend, Camilla, someone who's trying to help. You won't get away with it. I know you've had your little schemes in the past, but, Camilla, I just about shut the television off when I saw that. I just about shut—

The letter was unfinished. I've kept it since. I don't know why, besides feeling sentimental over what I suspect was the last thing she wrote, given the date, and my memory of her rambling obsession during the last three months of her life, which revolved entirely around Camilla Augustine of *Love & Life*—who, incidentally, was played by Loretta Juanez after her stint as Vivienne LaRoque on *Paradise Bluffs*.

And maybe that's some of it, part of it—my infinite pity for Vivienne LaRoque—twinkling nostalgia over old Mother Penny. But then, there's more: it's the lengths that Vivienne would go to to avenge herself on the Callister family for being excluded from the Callister family. Like if we could all be as equally unwilling to let go of things in life, of people and events, and pursue singular thoughts and wishes as though nothing else mattered, as though there wasn't money to earn, there wasn't art to market, there wasn't glory beyond the idea of glory, there was only this one thing at a time and it was both insane and expected that we should pursue it—maybe then life could be simple and satisfactory. Simple not only because it would give life moment-to-moment purpose, simple because it would be emotion distilled into action, running with the idea, or half of one.

Vivienne LaRoque—scorned woman, whose scorn exists as a way to give depth to her evil, intrigue to her disappointment—kidnapped the child of her ex-lover and his new wife, Juliana. She named the child Amelia, and, with the help of her deeply devoted friend and servant Dorian, raised the child up. It was only when Vivienne tried to use Amelia as a tool to get back her ex-lover (Phillip Callister, no less) that the truth was suddenly revealed over the course of several months, and Amelia, as a teen, was left to live with her real parents. Alone with Dorian, Vivienne realized that she had cared for the girl, that the girl was more than a means to an end, that she loved Amelia and Amelia loved her. They continued to see each other, to the disappointment of the Callisters, and life twisted like this. Vivienne seemed to continually have a scheme which would win for her the patriarch and doom Juliana to obscurity in a cave or hidden cell, and don't I want to lead a life of such purpose? To love and have it not be small and petty. Hank and I just fell into each other, and I suspect if I'd ever pursued him with murderous devotion, he'd have closed the door and returned to his recliner in the centre of the living room.

***

The state of my house isn't entirely my fault. I don't normally litter the floor with food wrappers. I've become absorbed by fast-food drive-thru transcription files and the robots at the window. I listen, I write what I hear, my appetite is aroused and, by the nature of sawdust-stuffed burgers, never sated. Though no one records my stimulated wish. If they did, we might become lost in a hall of mirrors of invented desire, i.e., demand for fish burgers is up tenfold among order typists typing orders for marketing meetings. Behavioural changes in the takeout-typing-transcriptionist population have led to an increase in the purchase of breakfast sandwiches while hand-pie numbers remain unchanged. Behaviourally changed typists—referred to hereafter as BCTs, pronounced jargonally as "bic-tiss"—are studied badly but nonetheless in order to discover a) the parameters of their stimulated desire, and b) what model can be generated from those parameters. Any insights are strictly intra-Quickburger, and while we hire stats grads and marketing majors, we don't check their grades. Is the key to the BCTs found in genetic disposition? If so, how can we determine the phenotype? Is the key to the BCTs found in the environment of the BCTs? If so, how can we determine personal affiliations? Given that breakfast orders are high among BCTs, what can we do to improve dessert appeal?

SURVEY: Please answer the following questions in order to have your name entered into a contest in which you could win a $5 Quickburger gift certificate:

1. Do you currently have or have you ever had breast cancer?

2. Do you listen to country-and-western music?

3. Do you prefer ice cream with a spoon or off the tongue?

What do I know about *why* I want? I transcribe the order, a strange one: fish sandwich, specified fresh, an order of oatmeal, and a dipped cone. Piqued by the process, I buy a cheeseburger. The orders that make up the files are usually under a minute long. They begin with the sound of a person sitting in their car; a low hum or a sputtering rattle can tell you much. They face a menu and a screen, sounds of background radio on their car speaker. The robot begins, "Welcome to Quickburger. What can I get for you?" With an irritable plea, the car dweller might ask, "Can I speak to a human?" To which the placid robot, almost aggressive in her flat reply, answers, "Okay. Can I get anything else for you?" Only to be met with cries of frustration and insistence that he didn't order whatever has now appeared on the screen. I can't imagine that the she-robo would let the screen register his request, let alone what she'd charge for a human, given that when anyone even asks for a spicy QuickChicken she denies them the possibility. "That customization is not available." But maybe we can find you something flesh.

***

I've increased my trips to the Savery. My kitchen-table desk and worn floral seat cushions could use the break. I'll sit on the plastic chairs of the Savery cafeteria—an uninviting bus station of a non-room for all the ambient action—and stare at the clip art on my foam cup: a whimsically askew blue-and-green teacup emitting scent lines and coffee beans on a background of flat waves and amoeba-like nothings, giving an impression of what looks like might sound like generic Latin muzak. No words on the cup. Nothing to read or see or do while I wait.

Near the window sits a panicked-looking mid-thirties man with dark hair and a limp tie. He looks into a black box, then out the window. He looks down. He looks up. His movements are jerky and reptilian. Vacant face like you shouldn't speak to him, or couldn't if you wanted to. Don't disturb the man with the phone. He's clearly experiencing something. Clearly coordinating something. Clearly creating or attempting to undo some spectacular or stupid happening.

And though I've heard tell of their wonders, Hank and I were peevish holdouts in the world of cellular phones. From the get-go.

"You've got a computer. You've got a home phone. You don't need another damn gadget," one of us said to the other. Which one to whom in what circumstance, I can't recall.

But anyway, it's just another appendage to pull around. And I do have my computer—a portable model I've considered lugging from kitchen table to mini-cafeteria to set up alongside Marigold's position as self-checkout helper so that I might wait for other files on her case and still not miss the possibility that she appears and speaks and fills out the her of her. Though what do I want with her? That's not the point. The point is the focus, the knowing, the uncovering, and it isn't even conscious, not really; well, it is, but it isn't anything I can control. It lingers. This feels like the thing I'm supposed to do, like the only thing I'm supposed to do, the only thing I get anything from now. I know what Marigold's father has done, and I'm sure I know how Marigold feels. But what will she say to the courts? What will her mother say? What will the ruling be? And how will she recover? Maybe I don't care; when I lay it all out, it just seems like someone else's soap. Yet another Christie Callister dragged through the mud.

But something about the proximity. The story is tantalizing, shamefully so, and that she's nearby creates around the beautiful girl an air of fame, celebrity. All the more so when I find out what a cunt her mother really is.

***

It's like a personal triumph and gift from God to see another Feeling file pop up after hours, or maybe days, of refreshing—relying, hardly, on a suspect email notification system. But quick, refresh and click on the row that contains the sorted names and states the rate that can be claimed for typing out the file, and you get a preview of the file. Always start with the preview. You never know what you're getting. The file could claim hearability at 95 per cent and halfway through the whole thing might turn to static and song. You can always unclaim the file, but if you unclaim too many, you might either earn a bad rating or just waste your time when you could've been searching for or typing out or cyberstalking others. So I start listening to the preview of this fresh Skontac Feeling file, and I know I have to be quick or someone else will claim it. I have only a small window. I should claim this one right away. I've been waiting for it.

But I wait more. I listen to the first ten seconds. It's habit. I have to make sure I want them—these voices, those voices. I know them; I come to know them with how close I listen, waiting for them to say "um," waiting for someone to interrupt [crosstalk]. I hear the betrayal in their voices, the way they get loud and dominate or become quiet and overwhelmed. Little sneers and breaths, and this one is unsure and that one is too sure—thinks he's important, becomes important. I have my judgments, my investments, my favourites. So I wait for the best voices, and I learn my taste in knowing, in being. It isn't rational; it isn't logical. I let this latent instinct lead the way now that I have nothing leading the way—fuelled by interest, curiosity, the feeling of possibility. A tribal restructure. Everything all at once leading you, and you it, toward the thing it is and the thing you are becoming—gangs of augmented intuitions, expanded, amplified; piecemealed psyches inhabiting multiple places at once, cracked and split along circuits, flying by on the radio waves. I'm in it for the titillation, the gossip. A perverted in-group trick now immoral, everything immoral by rules dished haphazard, rules determined by life at dead ends and commercial joy and deep and real feeling. When framed properly, we indulge; with proper qualification, you can be an amateur true crime detective, or within a socio-historical perspective, for knowing, for learning, for being of use to the public, you can use a search engine on a serial killer. But titillation and any underlying depravity are not to be encouraged or publicly admitted. If you serve your child up, you may find yourself unsated beneath a deceitful fruit tree.

Mona Deleanor is defensive. This is apparent from the first word she speaks, simply the way she says her own name. I can see her permed head wobbling and her eyes half closing, "Mona."

Amber Goodwin: Full name, please, Mona, and date of birth.

Mona Deleanor: [we don't transcribe the sighs] Mona Deleanor. April 6.

Amber Goodwin: Sorry, Mona, we need the full date.

Mona Deleanor: [we don't transcribe sneers or muttering] April 6, 1983.

Amber Goodwin: All right. So, I know this is difficult. And I want you to know that if you need someone to talk to, someone besides me, a counsellor, or... Just let us know and we'll end the...

Mona Deleanor: I don't need to talk to anybody. I can tell you everything I know about this right now. And that is fuck-all.

Amber Goodwin: Okay, you were not, and are not, aware of anything going on between your husband and your daughter?

Mona Deleanor: [we don't transcribe attitude] As I said, I don't know anything.

Amber Goodwin: Okay, okay. We're, just... We are required to follow up on this, to investigate. We've spoken to your husband already and we'll be speaking with your daughter as soon as we can arrange the meeting with HopeHouse-

Mona Deleanor: What house?

Amber Goodwin: HopeHouse is a service that pairs a counsellor with a victim and asks non-leading questions in a more comfortable environment. Not everyone is comfortable in... [laughs]. [we don't know if they gesture disappointedly around a small off-white room filled with coffee cups and sticky table rings, so we don't write it]

Mona Deleanor: Oh. Well, I'm just telling you, there's nothing, there's nothing I can say.

Amber Goodwin: Okay, okay, that's fair. Just to be clear, this is because you didn't witness anything? You were not aware of any behaviour between your husband and your daughter?

Mona Deleanor: Not aware. Not aware. What is it...like, any time they were close to each other? What do you want...I'm supposed to...what?

Amber Goodwin: Okay. For example, one of the incidents took place on the couch in the living room. Doug said you were at the store at the time and when they heard your car, they got up and got dressed.

Mona Deleanor: What are you asking?

Amber Goodwin: Just, when you came in-

Mona Deleanor: I didn't notice, I didn't see, I don't know. I really don't. I really don't.

Amber Goodwin: Okay, and that's fine, that's normal. That is totally normal. We just want you to know that we have people if you want to talk, and that you can contact us if you think of anything.

Mona Deleanor: I won't.

Amber Goodwin: Okay, okay. I know this can be difficult-

Mona Deleanor: Yeah.

Amber Goodwin: Okay.

The file cuts. Sometimes the file goes on and you must hear and transcribe the crew—something the customer can't want—little comments, stutters, missed jokes, guffaws—but the DERG org must have or else you'll lose points, and the more points you lose, the less files you get, and the less files you get, the less of a chance you'll ever find the end of any story. Or earn enough fifty centses to do whatever you do with your fifty centses.

Of course, *The Bluffs* is often available, in detail, on fan forums; every plot line will be safely and satisfactorily transcribed. Though, when it's within reach, I'm not sure why I lose interest. Why I search and follow up on cut scenes, on plot lines recently transcribed, and then abandon the quest, no longer curious about whether or not Ted, Tim, and Thomas Kinder's real father is Darius Landover, which he has to be—why else would they introduce the possibility, and what other use could their mother, Divinia, have to the overall story if Darius isn't the triplets' real father? Or else, maybe they're priming for a near-incest twist—Ted and Andrea—but they rarely go full incest on these shows. The suggestion, the possibility, exists just to offer that bit of titillation, an ache that can never be soothed, for it would be irredeemable and, thus, untellable. They'd have to kill the characters. So if the triplets' father is Darius, and Andrea Wesley, as it turns out, was given up for adoption by Cicilia Landover, Ted and Andrea would only be step-siblings and it wouldn't really be incest. That's probably where this whole thing's going.

I could follow up, I could weigh in, but I don't feel Russian soap fandom has really embraced me.

***

I wake up in the night. Swarming wordless urges and aches. It's 3:00 a.m. I'm sweaty. Shamble toward the supernal 7-Eleven on my kitchen table. Doors never locked, lights always buzzing. Horrors hanging from the hooks—a grinning medley of unrecoverable scrap and plastic arranged as invitation. My head is full; my bed is empty. My eyes grow wide. I'm soothed and irritated, heart-gut swap at the sound of the fan.

Type till my elbows ache and my fingers claw.

Like rummaging through a stranger's pockets, I'm greedy for something personal.

Two-minute instructional: How to Make Heart-Shaped Quilting Blocks.

Forty-five-minute debate between a rabbi, a priest, and an imam. Neither funny nor illuminating. "A cult like any other," Hank hollers in my ear while I shush shush shush him till he leaves and I screech into the dark echo of my empty house that he should come back, *come back*.

I unclaim a file featuring two rude girls laughing caustically and dismissing a world in which they show a dilettante's interest. Like me but louder, younger, and more fertile. I can't stand them.

I imagine myself watching the sun rise. I make a cup of coffee and sit on the front porch. But it's too early and too cold. I take my coffee back to the kitchen table.

Kat Lacassian: It's interesting, this IP you've acquired—it's from a newspaper, am I right?

Carl Hasapis: That's right, Kat. When the story about the telenovela Merry Maria came across our desks, we couldn't believe we'd never heard it before. And the really fascinating part of the story, to the whole team here at MindAnnihilator Studios, was how the show affected one town in particular.

Kat Lacassian: San Aquiles?

Carl Hasapis: [laughs] Kat, you read our press release. The series premiered in 1986 and was about a young girl who came from nothing and had to fight her way to the top of the horse-racing world. Classic rags-to-riches story. Limited series, ran for about four seasons. But just a massive hit across Latin America. Partly owing to the fact that they filmed in the small town of San Aquiles in southern Mexico.

Something about the story resonated throughout the region. It was a huge hit. And the article we read... I can detail this because we've wrapped filming, we've released the trailer, this thing is coming out in September. But the story we read about Merry Maria isn't just about this phenomenon of a TV show. Basically, when Maria was about to marry Gustavo, the stable boy who'd helped her win her championship and had always been there for her, the entire town of San Aquiles showed up. It was a fictional wedding, but the people of San Aquiles brought real presents, real rice... They took it seriously.

Kat Lacassian: Okay, I would totally do that, bring real rice to a fake wedding.

Carl Hasapis: [laughs] So, further down the rabbit hole. Initially, the priest who was supposed to marry Maria and Gustavo, who was a real priest, by the way, he refused to do it. But the studio promised to renovate his church...new roof, patch the holes, the whole nine yards. The priest agreed. And the wedding is huge, people are crying in the streets, it's massive. Bacchanalia. The party gets out of hand. On the third day of festivities, there's a riot at the local cantina. Two men and a horse are shot dead in the street, and the priest is excommunicated from the Catholic Church.

Kat Lacassian: Because of the riot?

Carl Hasapis: Well, in our version, it's because of the riot, because of the murders. I think in the newspaper they just described the excommunication as being due to the fake wedding. In the comic version made by Jules Camrose, amazing adaptor...we use him a lot at MindAnnihilator...he attributed the priest's excommunication to the wedding, the riot, as well as some hints of misappropriated funds. See, Kat, with non-fiction, you want to fit it to a fictional story structure. Like, does it satisfy that structure in a good way? And once we had the life rights of the priest...

Kat Lacassian: You met the priest?

Carl Hasapis: We had to. It was the only way we could be sure we wouldn't be sued. We had the IP from the newspaper, but the priest was a whole different story. IP is incredibly complicated. So yeah, we went down to San Aquiles, we found the excommunicated priest, we saw the church. We couldn't get the locals to really speak on the events. I think the excommunication of the priest was a turning point in the town, no one really wanted to talk about *Merry Maria* or the fallout from the riot, and we didn't want to retraumatize the town just because we felt like this was something interesting and marketable.

Kat Lacassian: Right.

Carl Hasapis: So we got the IP, the life rights, and we're just taking some liberties, you know? It's not really about *Merry Maria* anymore. We changed a lot of names, we made sure to not make it exploitative. We made the story ours. We're not interested in hurting the people of San Aquiles, but we are interested in good IP. In this climate, you can't pass up good IP.

Kat Lacassian: That's so interesting. What do you think it is about certain media... I mean, we've seen comic books, video games, even news stories and feeds being adapted, and it seems to go in both directions... It's this almost, like...well, not literally a snake eating its tail, but it's being developed in both directions. You're getting things that were in one form converted to another...

Carl Hasapis: There's just so much opportunity right now. Like, when we get good IP, we want to cradle-to-grave it...comic books, movies, bobbleheads, board games, video games, T-shirts, baby clothes, wallpaper, watches, screen-printed adult diapers, you know what I mean? So we have this story about a show, about the fallout after a show, about how life-changing it was, and that's how we feel about our show, you know what I mean? That's how invested we are. Like, yeah, it is like... I think I know what you mean, the ouroboros. We take it, make it, reinterpret it for every medium. So it isn't really a tail, it's like a spiral, or like the snake is eating its own tail and, like, growing or turning into something...

Kat Lacassian: Like the guy...the *Dune* sandworm?

Carl Hasapis: IP is the god emperor.

Kat Lacassian: Oh, I love that.

Rootless offerings on a hot-dog roller. Not nutritious but glistening, mouth-watering. And it won't kill you; you can live on it. You can forget there was ever anything different. It's easy to forget something you never knew.

Hank knew stuff. He read the paper. He knew an adequate version of what he needed to know. About now, about then. He'd look at the books, audiobooks, magazines, and instructional guides I'd take out of the library—take out and let linger on the kitchen table: *Crochet 101*, *The Basics of French*, *Cold Killers of the Canadian North*, *American Rose*, *Cat Fancy*, *World History for Dummies*, *Born to Bead*, *Wildflowers of the West*, *Buster's Old Book Value Guide*, *Classic Canadian Dishes*, *Microwave Cooking Volume 31*, et cetera, over time, through time.

"Pick something, Norma. Stick to something."

"I stuck to you."

Hank's eyes roll backwards.

I know enough. I *can* know so I might as well *already* know. The ease and speed make all of it somehow worthless, and the thing I should have been after—when I was grunting at my love and sucking at the bait—was what I already had. But I overreached; I threw myself out. *Stay alive*—I tell those sniggering little twits from an unclaimed podcast about "cultural issues"—*stay in love*.

I check my work, submit my service, and watch two episodes of *Merry Maria*. Entertained and paid. Amused and useful. 9:00 a.m. Sleep and generate dream.

***

"Vivienne is terrible," says user Cleo on a browser-translated version of a villains of *Paradise Bluffs* thread on tv.tb.ru. "Almost she redeemed herself by helping Amelia when blackmailed by Derek DeMarco, but then returned to scheming and attempt to kill Julianne."

"Ya, not good villain," Poolitchli87 chimes in. "Ugly. Boring."

They don't like Vivienne. They hate Derek. Derek I understand. He's controlling; he's demanding, greasy, weasel-faced. He was never scorned, never deceived. His impulses are his motivation. He seduced and impregnated Amelia in order to use their son Jason as leverage, as if that would make her love him and leave Thurston. Thurston, Derek, Amelia, Vivienne, Dorian, Mona, Marigold, Doug—they live in my mind like language.

There aren't enough files to create public demand, public engagement, and thus, a thread on the Deleanor plot. I know Doug is hurt—hurt himself, hurt his family—I could hear it in his voice. He must have a pitiable backstory. Poolitchli87 might say, "It's no excuse." Might even say that about Vivienne. And they're right, but I don't want excuses.

A good villain has nothing to do with outcome, with consequence. A good villain is good because he looks good, because he has beauty, allure, intrigue. Some villains are not villains, but distracted or single-minded opportunists. Does intention or lack of intention matter in the crafting of a good villain? Does the cunningness of their crimes? Does their passion? Passionate Amelia! Fan favourite. She lied to Thurston, wholesome Thurston with the sandy hair and white, white teeth! Thurston worships Amelia, trusts her—and yet, we root for *her*. Thurston should take *her* back. The evidence is in; the Russians have spoken. "She is, I think, most beautiful," says Svetlana01 on the worth of Amelia. Beauty, the real money. Vivienne's shrill face, brittle red hair, and scheming squint eyes make her villainy certain, set, but not appreciated. And yet Amelia sees something in her! When it seemed like the end for Amelia, when it seemed like Derek was about to expose everything, Amelia sought solace in the arms of her faux mother, Vivienne, who she believed was her real mother until she was a teenager and to whom she could reveal everything. Evil characters never judge other evil characters; they just try using the threat of revelation as part of their own evil plan. There's freedom in evil.

✳✳✳

When transcription is slow, I do the HITs. I signed up easy and decided I can click as well as I can type as well as I can answer questions or write questions or identify furniture as furniture, doors as doors, and pick from a pile my favourite artificial face. HUMAN INTELLIGENCE TASKS—anybody can do. Join a world in which students, scientists, and marketeers pay pennies for input and where one can click around for pennies for output and see for what the world is looking. Gather and sell and take the fractured extensions toward a white noise of unity—little collected bits and bots amass like a god then—a plundering warted god, a massive breathing chittering thing. I can't say it isn't strange, and I can't say it's stranger than anything else, but occasionally the absurd poetry of the entire abstraction strikes me as utter. I am gutted, as they say.

HIT: Determine the Truth of the Following Statement:

CONTEXT: A woman and a dog work through an agility course.

STATEMENT: The dog is dead.

IS THIS STATEMENT TRUE, FALSE, OR NEITHER?

What is conjured in this effort to determine whether or not I reason, pitted against the reasoning skills of perhaps a computer or small piece of a computer? A woman sadly dragging her bloodied dog through a ramshackle obstacle course. The hope the dog once held and the broken limbs she places with deluded persistence through the heaves of her chest, against the catwalk, strike everyone as depraved. FALSE within this horrific and punily far-fetched scenario. Of course, intelligence isn't determined by irrational absurdity. Not yet.

✱✱✱

Marigold, living like normal, looking even joyful in the grocery store, needles me. I go daily and drink coffee and wait for something to be revealed or else to see evidence of impact or illness. And Doris comes over and they just talk about how busy the store is or sometimes they talk about the slackers in the floral department. Marigold smiles and I'm strangely vexed. As though I know she has too much on her mind and this isn't the response I'd presume comes next in the thing of things. Shouldn't she always be dwelling and weeping and scheduling meetings and going to court? And if her mother never noticed, I wonder, with self-reproach, about the behaviour on Marigold's part that made normalcy out of perversion. She hugged him; she was always hugging him. What was she thinking? Nothing is her fault—it couldn't be, I know that—but I sometimes wonder at the innocence of children. Children who test their limits and the limits around them. Children who invent rules to avoid the reality of their dependence. Who break out of expectation to say they've broken it and damn themselves against their own interests. Little fools.

That's why Hank and I never had kids. Is it? I don't know; it just never came up. I must be sterile. I must be cold and sterile and uncaring and inhuman. We just consumed; we didn't create. Nothing. Watched. The news, what's on. When we worked, we were busy, and we'd spend sort of peaceful but uneventful evenings together or at Margery's or visiting with his mother. And my whole family has been dead for so long they hardly count as family. My parents died when I was young. They were old. My father had a heart attack, and my mother was hit by a bus. The bus incident might not be related to age, but she was a pretty slow walker, so there was a variety of factors. I got my father's insurance payout, met Hank, got my mother's insurance payout, married Hank. We bought a house. Hank worked as a supervisor in a janitorial supply factory until he retired. I don't know what else I can say about it. Kids didn't come up. We didn't think of kids. We didn't even think of each other. It all fell, dominoes.

Did we make any choices? Sure. I gave my mother a pine casket. We bought the cheapest shampoo. We both had dandruff and neither addressed it. And in all that time, the death of Hank's mother, Penny, caused the first real rift. He went wild. He was always gripping me and asking me questions about who I called, about collecting her things from the home, about the mail, the weather, the menu. In the things I would've handled on my own, he became too interested. He was pushing at me. Scratching at me. But we still had Margery then, and she always calmed me down, gave me some Earl Grey and gin, and we chuckled about this and that, you know. About the news or about whichever show. I never did watch soap operas then—though I'd nearly kept up through Penny's recaps—but I felt busy, busy with life, though what life was I can only guess about now. I was talking. Making lunch plans. Buying provisions. I don't feel bad, but I suppose I never thought about how I felt. I just am; I just was, the ivy growing up the bookshelf.

***

Juliana Callister I can't stand. She's wholesome; she's airy. She's always waving her blond head around. I wonder why they don't pursue blind hatred on this show. Vivienne LaRoque needn't hate Juliana for stealing her husband; Vivienne could hate Juliana for being so good, so implacable. So moral. A person who always feels the right thing, always does the right thing. Who can *stand* that? Everyone, I guess, because she's beloved. A crowd favourite. She was on *The Bluffs* until it ended in the early nineties, did a brief run on *Young Passion*, and she's been touring the soap cons ever since, same haircut, same soft lighting. A woman who carries soft lighting with her into the world should be beloved, surely. And yet, as she exists in this and as that, I wish her failure. Spitefully, malevolently, I embrace Vivienne.

What a world! Who am I that I can't love the person and know the person, that I act vengefully and spitefully and aesthetically? I must be godless. I must be godless. Up the bookshelf and around the books I never read, I extend, in domesticated soil.

***

HIT: Determine the Truth of the Following Statement:

CONTEXT: A man in torn pants plays a broken violin while sitting on a bucket on a wharf on the Atlantic Ocean.

STATEMENT: The man is not wearing pants.

IS THIS STATEMENT TRUE, FALSE, OR NEITHER?

Don't you get it, torn pants are pants. They're still pants. At what point do pants stop being pants? When they're shorts, when they're rags, when they're a pair of culottes? But the context determines the statement, and if the pants are said to be worn, no matter how ragged they are, the pants remain worn. Time is not specified. The wharf is there to distract you. See beyond the man. We only want his pants.

***

I was what's called a miracle baby. My parents didn't expect me. My mother expected menopause. They're old in my memories. Old and polite. We were like friendly acquaintances. I have an impression of a curtsy, though it's unlikely I ever gave one. I felt I was accepting their hospitality, and when the day came, graduation or marriage, a debt would be paid, a kindness run its course, and we'd all shake hands and separate amicably.

It wasn't quite. My father, the upright Mr. Shandling, surprised the world with his death as he never had with his life. He used to walk briskly to work each morning. He managed a local bank, the same bank he'd always worked at. He swept the floors as a teenager, cashed cheques as a young man, and eventually he moved in. His lunches were balanced: he ate apples and chicken sandwiches, sometimes egg or fish. He didn't even drink coffee. He drank water, and soda on the weekends, as a treat. His heart attack was ridiculous. We would've all assumed his heart was the tip-toppest among us. A rigid, particular, perfectly hatted man. He was over sixty, and you can't live forever, but, well, we all would've thought longer. Mother, the admirable Mrs. Shandling, took it rather poorly. I remember I made a gesture, I moved toward her, I said, "Mama," strangely, as it wasn't something I'd ever called her, but the moment—I thought the moment called for it. And she didn't take note of my gesture or my *Mama* with anything like surprise or disgust or even affection. She politely nodded and closed her eyes. She kept them closed for only a second and then smiled a very small tight smile and closed the door to her bedroom and never really came out.

I'd just graduated high school, and before Mr. Shandling's demise I'd been thinking, *I should be leaving*, but after, it seemed like my duty to stay. I had nowhere else to go anyhow. I had no real plan for my life. But when Mrs. Shandling cut me a cheque for a lump sum of Mr. Shandling's insurance payout, she did so with an air of finality. I wanted to ask what she'd do now, who she'd make lunches for, what kind of old woman she'd be, alone. But the moment was never right. I couldn't make it right. It was too quiet in her house. At least Father Shandling played news radio. Mama Shandling, she just seemed to tidy in near silence, a gentle clack—her black heels on the linoleum. I thanked my mother for the amount and rented a little place in town. It wasn't final. I knew my duties: I visited on Sundays, and she made lovely—really with loveliness that I failed to carry on—lovely little sandwiches. And I told her about my waitressing job, about my rough customer who was visiting me more often. I told her of my life, and I bade her goodbye. Nothing was missing.

***

NOTIFICATION: Your favourited user UJANG FEELING has submitted another file. Would you like to claim it now?

Marigold's grandmother, though you can't tell from paper—we don't write out sound effects, onomatopoeia, gentleness—Marigold's grandmother is a real grandmother. She's creaky and sweet and cries, "Ohh, oh my, oh my goodness," like her big, crinkled heart is cracking.

But DEATH—it seems now that I mean to compare my life to Marigold's—mine is marred by the repetition, the constancy of death—the death of my grandparents before I knew them, my parents before I knew them, my own ingrown family after I'd known them, overknown them—

"People die," Hank said when Margery's metastatic breast cancer ate her up and killed her quick. Then he cried. I'd never seen him cry. He didn't cry when his mother died, when our two yowling Siamese cats died—he snorted then, when one cat died, then the other, a strange snort of relief and missing, a lack, a hole where an unwanted thing once lived, a bad neighbour who'd had his moments. He didn't ever cry—so what? I didn't think it was strange. It was strange when he did cry. A big, fat, blubbering cry. "People die." Blubber blubber sniff panic.

I wish I had felt the right thing then; I wish I'd comforted him with real affection. I'd felt sick. Like I wanted to get away. I'd been crying myself, a silent sniffling cry. I'd been crying in the bedroom, sitting on my side of the bed, feeling the slightly slippery embroidered salmon-coloured bedspread beneath my shapeless dress—my shoes on, my hair fluffed. I perked my face up and patted some little bits of powder from a small compact so the pink blotches wouldn't make me unsightly. Before what? Before who? Well, I don't know. Surely he thought after—what was it then, forty-five years? forty-six?—that he could cry a big fleshy thick-lipped snotting gulping cry; surely he thought he could do that in front of me even though I'd never done that in front of him, and what I'd do was what he needed: I'd love him more, I'd love him at all. I'd offer everything he was missing. I'd suck it out of him, the sick feeling, the hollow longing feeling. But I hugged him like an aunt, a great-aunt, a distant great-aunt who'd never known anything more about his life than what was sent in letters. He shut up after that. And though I tried to go to him later, with a roast dinner, with no complaints, he must have known how incomplete we were. Or not. Maybe not—

But DEATH—my grandparents all died when I was very young. There's a picture of me as a baby, wearing a little blue dress and little blue shoes, holding the hand of an ancient woman while she sits in a rocking chair. I'm small, maybe two, just beyond baby, I should say toddler, and my hand is reaching up toward her hand, which dangles limply alongside the chair. This was my mother's mother, Gladys. So I knew her, but I really can't say I knew her. As much as I knew the baby in blue near an antique wooden chair holding an antique wooden lady. I am not the toddler stranger, me not me. This picture can't mean anything. *Strange*, I think, *strange*. But anyway, they were all dead by the time I was old enough to remember anything about living and changing. I wonder if they would've believed me as wholly and endlessly as Marigold's grandmother believes Marigold. I wonder if they would've wept and torn at their white hair over their awful son, their wretched boy. Does Marigold know what she has in Rosa?

***

HIT: Determine the Truth of the Following Statement:

CONTEXT: A brown-haired woman wearing denim feeds the pigeons in the park.

STATEMENT: A woman in blue surrounded by birds.

IS THIS STATEMENT TRUE, FALSE, OR NEITHER?

True. It really must be.

***

Laeticia Matthers is saccharine. She repeats "of course, of course" with such frequency I imagine that if she has a stroke it'll go unnoticed because of the convenient rhythm of her tick-like words. But I'm sure if I was in the room with Rosa Deleanor and Laeticia Matthers from ye ole HopeHouse, I'd find Matthers soothing, reassuring, and necessary. She's trying to calm and comfort Rosa, doing what she's supposed to do. Rosa speaks to Laeticia about Marigold and about her son Doug. And Rosa tears at her skin. There's something about the distance between me and Laeticia, though, that makes me suspicious of her summoned empathy, her service-industry empathy—a civic empathy people so often mistake for real interest and compassion, forming their identities around polite positive feedback, the feigned interest of employees and sham mothers who kiss the spot where hard cement fails to break the skin. But Rosa pays no mind to the sham, knowing—you can hear it in her voice, a weary well-accustomed-to-tragedy voice—exactly who she is. I believe in Rosa, in her tears, laments, in her life and history. So why not extend that same feeling to Laeticia with her warbling voice and affected heartfeltery?

Laeticia Matthers: Any time, Rosa, any time you feel you can't go on, okay, just tell me, tell me and we'll end the session. It's that easy. It's just that easy.

Rosa Deleanor: My dear, I don't terribly want to even begin the session.

Laeticia Matthers: Of course, of course. Should we reschedule then? Should we do this another day? What do you think, Rosa? Can I call you Rosa?

Rosa Deleanor: I'd imagine. No, no, let's begin. What can I tell you?

Laeticia Matthers: All right. Okay, good. Okay. Were you aware of any inappropriate conduct between your son and your granddaughter? Between Doug and Marigold?

Rosa Deleanor: I can't say I was aware. No, I can't say that.

Laeticia Matthers: All right. All right. Did you ever notice strange behaviour between Doug and Marigold?

Rosa Deleanor: Strange... Oh...I don't know, it wasn't that I noticed. But...Mari seemed... Oh my, oh... I just don't know... I felt like Mari was different, had changed. But I didn't know. I don't know. Teenagers are different. She was quiet, her eyes looked dark...no, what does that mean, she looked...nervous? Not really nervous... Can we come back to this question? I just...

Laeticia Matthers: Of course, of course. Sure, yes. Of course, of course. Are you aware of any strange behaviour by your son Doug?

Rosa Deleanor: [laughs sadly; transcriber leaves this out] Doug, my boy. Oh, oh my goodness... Yes, Doug...he had a difficult life. I don't know why. I tried, I did try. His stepfather, he was rough with the boy, and Doug, I guess he was sensitive. I don't know, I didn't really say anything. I'm only saying it now because so much time has passed and I can look at it or... But we...I thought we were normal. Though Doug was secretive. We found him... Well, this is... I don't want to say this...

Laeticia Matthers: Of course, of course. Let me know when you're ready.

Rosa Deleanor: He... Well, we caught him in the back yard. He must have been eleven or twelve. His stepsister, Randy's girl, Diane, she was a year or two older... We caught him—them, I should say. I don't know who did what to whom. They were raised together, siblings more or less, but of course they weren't really, and I didn't... I tried not to think about it. They were so young, we didn't think at the time they really knew what they were doing.

Laeticia Matthers: Yes, I understand. Yes, mm-hmm [affirmative], of course, of course, sure. And was that the only incident?

Rosa Deleanor: It all seems so much worse now, in light of Mari... But it happened so gradually. I don't know, I must have made excuses. He was a boy... And then, well, I lost track of him. When he was older, he did what boys his age did, I thought. He dated, he drank. I knew he drank...

Laeticia Matthers: But, so there were other incidents?

Rosa Deleanor: There was, well, we suspected something with his younger sister. I don't remember all the details, it was an impression, you see. I remember Randy and I...I remember sharing a look. There was this time that Linda, our youngest, Randy and I, our daughter together, there was this time that she, must have been five or six, came tearing into the kitchen. She had been with her brother, I guess he was thirteen or fourteen, I can't remember, and she just came running in. He came in after, telling us he had scared her. But she didn't look scared... And he had this smirk, this strange smirk...

Laeticia Matthers: Sure, of course, of course. Can you remember how she looked or what she said?

Rosa Deleanor: I don't know if a five-year-old can really look repulsed. But that's what I want to say. I don't know. I wish I knew. I wish I knew.

Laeticia Matthers: Of course, of course, yes, I understand. I do. And how are you feeling? Can we come around to the question of Marigold and Doug?

Rosa Deleanor: Well, maybe, you know what? Maybe it was the same, or similar. Or I don't know now what I remember and what I am rather...rather willing myself to think. But she, Mari, I mean, I think maybe that was it, she had an air of repulsion. Not like a teenager, not like a teen girl, not haughty, you know, I've had my own. But like...more pained... And Doug, you know, he laughed, he was always laughing things off. It was easy to not take anything seriously with Doug. He liked to drink, he liked to have fun, and he just... Doug, my boy, I do love him. Doug. Oh, oh my goodness... Oh...

Laeticia Matthers: Of course, of course. I'm just going to step out for a moment. You sit tight, Rosa. Can I get you anything? Water or anything?

Rosa Deleanor: I would take some tea, sweetheart.

Laeticia Matthers: Oh, unfortunately, it's just water or soda. We have this machine out here.

Rosa Deleanor: Water, thank you.

The file cuts. And I'm reminded of yet another file I transcribed a month or two ago. A file that filled me with the irritable realization, the fear, the sinking truth that good is not met with good and sense is not met with sense and the thing that accumulates is only an accumulation, a mass of likeness, or coupling of corrupted things. Listening to Rosa made me think of old Buck and warm and wise grandparents and the strange insincerity of everyone around them going about their business.

Though here I am, grandparent age, grandchildless, going about my business, being everything other than warm or wise, kindly or loving—but who is there to love? Hank, I sometimes miss the heat of him, the stink of him beside me like a sack of medical waste. Hank, what was he good for? The bum. And me, was I good for him? Don't think about it.

Anyway, there was this wildly idiotic transcription file that lingered in me for the dynamic revealed or the strangeness suggested of life outside of scripted life, that is, I bet, the bulk of life. It was this snotty kid, what can I say, he sounded fat and pale—an indoor boy. He sounded like a sneering little round face with skin that was too soft, like if you poked him slow and steady, your hand would be absorbed by his puckered whitish flesh. This fellow, who never introduced himself to the transcriber, interviewed his grandfather for reasons, I gathered, that had something to do with the end of WWII and his grandfather's time in the Korean War. The grandfather, the kid just called him Grandpa, but his name was listed in the instructions of the file as Buck. A good old name, a good old fella. This kid was asking Buck about his old pictures, pictures of Buck and his friends, friends from another time. They talked about the town in which he grew up and about his life as a boy, and the kid made the comment that these days there's hardly anyone who wears the clothes in these pictures, these old-fashioned clothes. He noted this, though, through an utterly needless insult: the boy asked Buck, with laboured humour and an undercurrent of menace, who the person at the end of the gang was: "Who's this lesbian on the end?"

"The what? Who?" Buck was confused, to the quick.

The kid went on with a soft, subtle jeer, "This one on the left, at the end? This one dressed like a lesbian?"

"No, what? This here on the end is Howard Zimmer, it was his brother, you remember, who died in Iwo Jima. That's Howie." Buck sounded like he'd already forgotten, like he was used to forgetting about the weird shit that not only his grandson said but that perhaps everyone often said. As though he was just always completely ready to forget about the weird shit that he couldn't assimilate, that couldn't be assimilated.

"Ohhh, Howie Zimmer. His brother, yeah. No one dresses like that anymore except lesbians."

"No, well, I wouldn't know about that," Buck told the boy matter-of-factly.

"How does it make you feel that lesbians have appropriated the all-American boy look?"

"I...I just don't know about that. I would say they can wear whatever, I'm not going to say they shouldn't."

"There's all this talk about cultural appropriation these days... It wouldn't bother you to know that lesbians walk around dressed like Howie Zimmer?"

Buck laughs. "I'm not going to talk about this anymore, this conversation is going nowhere."

The kid laughs too and redeems himself slightly before the scrutinous transcriber.

This hearty honesty I dredge up when I feel I only know what—blank. My boy Hank, I could talk about him endearingly, but what would it mean? I was no good. He was a man who shared my bed. But maybe if someone put it to me, "Tell me what it was like to sleep next to Hank," I could pull on, if only for show, and through show, make and attend the same show—be a believer: "Hank, he was mine, my old man." And face the interviewer, who was insincere, insane, reeking of agenda and pettiness—face them with the indifference of age, and something like wisdom.

***

I can see the glowing red Savery sign from my front porch. The other grocery stores are a bit farther. Two or three kilometres. It's a ways for me. I have heavy old legs and varicose veins. I can feel my waddle—aches but doesn't pain, throbs—and I don't like to think about it. But maybe a throbbing body is better than a spinning head. Sometimes I try to smile at the people on the streets, like an exercise in neither throbbing nor spinning—though it's a new smile or a forced smiled or a pained smile, and it's not comfortable. I've never had a comfortable smile. Not like Margery—who I sometimes thought that, had I not married into the family, wouldn't have bothered to know me. But time and age fit us together, I think. I think we fit together. She had a wide toothy smile. Her teeth were yellow, but that didn't seem to matter. Her whole face changed when she opened her mouth. Smiling and laughing came so naturally to Margery. Not really to Hank, who had more of a smirk, a raised eyebrow. And not really for me, who had, who has, only thin lips pressed together when she tries and a pained square hole of a laugh when something gets her going. Anyway, I put everything into it. I know what you're supposed to do when you're walking around. I know what an old lady should be. I'm sure I do. Sometimes I do. I press my lips together and strain my cheeks. I forget my body. I think of my face; then I think of their faces. Most people smile back. I think hideous thoughts about those who look away. The effort I put in! And they turn their heads, pretending not to notice, or else they really don't notice at all.

So today, I'll just go to the Savery. Winter is over, but it lingers into spring, and since it was cold and wet and foggy yesterday, hoarfrost grew overnight and covered the trees in a spiky jumble. By the early afternoon the wind had knocked much of it down, and now it swirls around the streets like shredded coconut spilled from the bag. It looks so silly and only as edible as shredded coconut—I'm dizzy with it. First it's joy, unbridled; I almost laugh squarely on the street under the spiny trees. And then this arid sickness sinks. It's not as though Hank would have cared about the snow on the streets and how it had, perhaps never, or at least infrequently, appeared to be shredded coconut spilled from the bag and scattered on the ground, but if I mentioned it to him, he would've looked. He would've been forced to see and even see it as I was seeing it if I could figure out a way to tell it to him properly. But that idiot is nowhere that he can hear me, and so, sick from too much coconut, I head to the grocery store just to have some coffee in the small section beside the self-checkout stands.

***

Marigold's alight. That's the only way I can think to say it. Like a little songbird landed. I try to figure out what she is. Maybe pulled from my own brain—yanked from the extra-extendibrains of others, of shoppers, familiar strangers. How do I know what I know, what I see—she must be sixteen or seventeen, I can't be sure, but her skin is smooth and her hair long and untangled. Her ears stick through her hair; I can see their small, pale tips. I can't understand where she keeps herself, how she keeps herself. I try to imagine her old—in her thirties, a newly withered bloom, the rosy blush of youth roughening into a weathered rosacea. Still beautiful, but no longer strange, no longer fascinating—in her fifties, white-haired, violet-eyed, but like many a former beauty, delicate in black and white, with a stunning red heel like an allusion to a self that wouldn't be forgotten, even if better off—ancient in her nineties, infirm, hunched; desperation in her pansy eye, longing for oneself and one's own memories to be relived, refreshed, or scratched, the blond girl not trapped but dead beneath a doddering sac of wizened skin. I think she sees me; I turn away. Were her brows low? Did her lips retract? Doris walks over to Marigold with her characteristic directness like a permed grocery nurse, nodding efficiently but not heartlessly, always making sure everything is on track, up to speed. "How did it go, dear? Are you feeling all right?" Doris asks, and from the side of my eye I can see the middle-aged woman's acrylic nail sparkling under the high and hazy electric lights. *How did it go? How did it go?* Marigold is silent. I'm crushing my emptied cup. *How did it go?*

"They were really nice. They were. I'm—I'm glad that part of it's done. It'll be a while before the court date. But at least, you know, at least I finally got to tell it. I feel like it's real now, if that makes sense." Marigold's words catch in her throat, and Doris holds the girl. Inappropriate! Doris, give the girl a break! Take the girl into the lunchroom! I look at them unbelieving, and again Marigold glances my way. I make for the exit.

***

Through the parking lot, a waddled rush, a strained huff of a rush: "Norma!"

It's a grey-haired man with thick glasses and inverted eyebrows.

"Norma, it's me, Ted." *Ted Kinder, triplet, son, lover.* "I used to work with Hank at, uh, EconoClean. We met, oh…at, uh, you know, one of the Christmas parties." He chuckles.

"Sure, Ted, sure, I remember you," I say, nodding and trying to keep forward motion, let's not dawdle, there are files to check, only so much time, it's probably too late, it's probably exactly the length of this man's intention too late.

"I was, uh, so sorry to hear about Hank's passing, Norma. You know, uh, I wish I could have made it to the funeral. I really do. I was out of town with the family. It was a stroke, eh?"

"Subarachnoid hemorrhage." I say it like I've rehearsed it, like another mouth rehearsed it for me, like that other mouth is saying it and I'm watching it be said. "I was at the store." Stiff. Otherworldly. An otherworldly misty thing, a flitting, floating *rush* escapes from the sidewalk, or maybe emerges from my feet, feet or concrete; something rises up, twirls my head, tingles my arms.

"Oh gosh, Norma, I'm so sorry. Just, uh, what? Sixty-five? Seventy?"

"Seventy-four," someone says. I say. My mouth opens and closes around the number.

"Still, too soon, too soon—"

"Had I been home," I hear myself mutter. "Time is brain." Are these words audible? I thought I was walking but I've stopped. What am I racing about for? What is the thing I needed to do? To get home, to get home.

"Huh." Ted nods slowly, a little perplexed. "So, uh, how have you been, um-uh, holding up, Norma?"

I sigh and silently gather myself up from some millisecond of incoherent violent emotion brought on, maybe, by the ums and uhs and incomprehensible phrases I'm unable to edit while watching him, this grey man flitting around a stunted sympathy. "I'm...I'm all right, Ted," I say. "Thanks for asking." Let it be over. It feels like something...like I can't find something—like I have secrets to keep and his aim is to get them out of me. Hank's friend. Hank's buddy. Old man or young hunk in love on TV alongside my favourite celebrity, Vivienne, Oh Viv—

"You know, Norma..." He grabs my arm with gentle firmness. I look at his tanned hand on my raincoat. "If I'd, uh, you know, been able to make it to the funeral, I would have stood up there at the podium, front of everyone, you know, never did that before, but, uh, and I woulda told the story about the time when ol' Hank ripped the seat right out of his pants. You must have heard this? You know, unforgettable. Me 'n' the boys never let him forget it. He was sitting down, you know, to eat there in the, uh, lunchroom—" he wheezes "—and there was this sound, cccccccccrrrrrrrrrrrraaaaahhhccc, like that, eh? This looooong draaaaaawn-out riiiiiiiiiiip! And, you know, there must have been an, uh, echo or whatnot in that lunch room, because everybody in the whole damn building heard it, swear to God! And, you know, Hank just shook his head, stood up, and, uh, you know what he shouted?"

I shake my head, no, no, I don't know. No.

"'Lord help me, get my wife!'" Ted raises his arms up in the air and affects a gruff Hank impersonation, then laughs.

"Hmfh." I breathe air through my nose and smile politely, while shaking, trying to shake the shiver out of me. I stutter, "Well, yep, yes, I did the cooking, the cleaning, the mending. I always did that."

He puts his hand on my arm again. "It isn't that, Norma, it's just... I mean... He really, uh, you know, appreciated you. *Norma this, Norma that.* I, uh, you know, I don't think he could have got on without you. The two of you, gosh, you just had this beautiful—" *expanding, affected emotion with his arms* "—traditional—" *it's a play for me, for my benefit* "—marriage." He puts his arms to his sides and re-laxes his face.

"Hmfh." I don't know if I know what he means. I've got a chill, I'm cold, I'm trapped.

"Oh, not in a bad way, Norma, no, uh, no, not at all, I mean, you know, it was a really beautiful thing you had. How long were you all married for?"

"Forty-seven years," I say, knowing now that I have to pull myself together and shut this thing down. Ted here is in a mood, high on coffee and his own chatter. If he keeps me much longer, I'll need to take *his* arm. "Well, it was good to see you, Tim—"

"Ted."

"Ted, of course, I'm sorry, I must have confused you with your brother. It was nice running into you. I should... I must... I have to get going." Unnatural insistence.

"I don't have a brother! But, uh, you take care, Norma," Ted says loudly, tightening his mouth in a clear and com-municable sign of care.

Now I have to recover. Now I have to warm up after that cold air shivered through me and travelled up me and made its way inside my head and all around my dark little heart. I'm cold. Gosh, I'm lost now. Yes, I remember when Hank brought me his pants to be mended, but the rip was bad, and they were done, fit for the trash. I didn't tell him we threw them out, but neither did he ask or much care. It's not the kind of thing I'd thought lived on in anybody's mind. But what plays now as I walk quickly away, is the four of us (neither Ted, Tim, nor Thomas) all hanging around: Hank in his chair, Penny and Margery at the kitchen table, and me, ironing off to the side of the two rooms, in an in-between area where I always ironed.

Margery called out to Hank, "Jesus hell, what d'you got her ironing your pants for, brother? It's the twenty-first century, can you not do it yourself?"

Hank turned from his seat, remote in hand, to reply, "Now, what would the good woman do if she were not ironing my pants?"

Margery rolled her eyes and sighed. Hank winked at me. I smiled. I smiled, he winked; he winked, I smiled; something in his eye, something in my teeth, shake it off. Never happened. What would I have done if I had not been ironing his pants? Like he knew. Like he gave me purpose. Like he was purpose. Like the useful part of me is dead. Dead 'n' gone. Not just the part that smiled, the part that winked, the part with knowledge, with facts, with know-how, the part that checked and protected, that kept safe and made sure all was done right, the part that wouldn't have stood for disorder, disarray. The part I resented. The part that doesn't get a real body with a real wink, with a real smell or a real heart. The part that's dead. An aimless fool remains. Free and unfettered. Free and formless. Walking around chilled from a life that should bring me joy, walking around wrinkled and greasy from ironing nothing and cleaning no one. Well, Ted, well, Tim, thanks for the memories, but they're just not pretty enough to make the cut. Thanks, fellas, but I think we should hear a little more about this Christie Callister business and what, exactly, you did or didn't do to her. Let's hear you weasel out of it again and again and again; rewind the tape, drag back the video progress bar; you're never getting out of this one.

∗∗∗

The phone is ringing. I can hear it from the porch. I fumble with my keys, clatter through the door, answer breathlessly. "Hello?"

"Hello. This is an automated service. I'm calling from SmartSmile Dental Care. Um, can you confirm that this is the phone number of, let's see, Henry Nimmo?"

"What is this about?"

"This is an automated service. I'm calling from Smart-Smile Dental Care. Um, can you confirm that this is the phone number of, let's see, Henry Nimmo?"

"I can't tell what this is. Is this a robot?"

"I'm calling from SmartSmile Dental Care."

"What is this?"

"This is an automated service."

"You sound just like a person. I don't know what they've done, but you sound just like a person."

"Um, can you confirm that this is the phone number of, let's see, Henry Nimmo?"

"Just what is this? What exactly is this?"

You have to say the next thing to get the game to go ahead, but I couldn't say it. I can't say the right thing. This must be a new service. At least the unnatural flatness of a recognizable robot's reply fits together with what *I'm* supposed to be, what *I* am in the world. Robotic robots and warm bank tellers preserve the illusion. Don't let them mimic human unsurety, scrounge for appropriate distance, insert word whiskers and fraternal jocularity, affect an off-the-cuff all-American boyish tone—what would Buck think of the dental-assisting robots affecting the all-American boy stylings of heroes like Howie Zimmer? Don't let them remind us that we can't remember the last time we were people and that with such distance between people and such presumption by false people we grow to affect that which we thought we were but have never really been. Alien or adapted? Both, likely, because, as they say, X is not a monolith—nice, for the pained shill who makes it through, but how it makes me sick to fall behind and watch the parts that get picked up, mutations that take and keep, and the horrid little winners flaunting yesterday's failure as today's well-earned successes. I'm not bitter, not bitter. No. Just old.

***

HIT: Determine the Truth of the Following Statement:

CONTEXT: There is a woman throwing daggers at a target, which is a carrot.

STATEMENT: An athletic woman is targeting carrots with a blade.

IS THIS STATEMENT TRUE, FALSE, OR NEITHER?

But what are they asking? But do they want to know whether it is generally true or precisely true? Dagger or blade? Can it be determined by the very act of throwing that she is at least moderately athletic? Oh, absurdity, as if it were more absurd to position a carrot as though it were a dagger itself facing the blade than to lay it flat on a table or pinned ridiculously sidelong to a tree; and as if it were more absurd to target a de-rooted vegetable over the tree itself, which is something of an oversized vegetable. How to determine the truth of things: eye on the prize: a carrot perched on a tree.

***

NOTIFICATION: Your favourited user UJANG FEELING has submitted another file. Would you like to claim it now?

Laeticia Matthers:	Hi, Marigold, so my name is Laeticia, I've been here at HopeHouse for a little over two years, okay? So this is my job, this is what I do, and I want you to feel comfortable, okay?
Marigold Deleanor:	Okay.
Laeticia Matthers:	Can I get you anything to drink?
Marigold Deleanor:	Is there, like, tea?
Laeticia Matthers:	Just pop and water, sorry.
Marigold Deleanor:	I'm okay.

Laeticia Matthers: Of course, of course. Okay, so, are we ready?

Marigold Deleanor: Okay.

Laeticia Matthers: Can we just start by getting you to state your full name and date of birth.

Marigold Deleanor: Marigold Rose Deleanor. February 2, 2005.

Laeticia Matthers: Great, great. Okay. So you currently live with your grandmother?

Marigold Deleanor: Yes.

Laeticia Matthers: Was there any particular reason that you moved in with your grandmother?

Marigold Deleanor: I guess...I just... We're just really close.

Laeticia Matthers: Of course, of course. So you weren't uncomfortable living at home with your parents?

Marigold Deleanor: Well...I don't know.

Laeticia Matthers: So can you tell me a little bit about living with your parents.

Marigold Deleanor: It's okay, I guess. My dad...

Laeticia Matthers: Your father, Doug?

Marigold Deleanor: Yeah, he's... I guess he, like, molests me and stuff.

Laeticia Matthers: Okay. Are you able to tell me what he does?

Marigold Deleanor: He just, like, touches me, I guess.

Laeticia Matthers: Can you recall any specific incidents?

Marigold Deleanor: There was the most recent, I guess... with my friend Krystal. I think I told the other lady about that.

Laeticia Matthers: Right, right. Are you able to talk about what happened exactly? Your father...

Marigold Deleanor: We were just all hanging out, I guess, on the bed...

Laeticia Matthers: You were in his...in the master bedroom?

Marigold Deleanor: Yeah. Well, like, we were just watching TV, he wanted to smoke weed and he had some in the bedroom. And we smoked a little bit and just watched, like, I think, that cop show, you know?

Laeticia Matthers: Hm, of course, of course, all right. Can you tell me what happened after that?

Marigold Deleanor: He was just, like, touching Krystal, kind of on the butt, and I guess he told us both to take our clothes off.

Laeticia Matthers: And you did?

Marigold Deleanor: Mm-hmm [affirmative]. Yeah, and then Krystal like...sucked his dick.

	And I... He just kind of touched me, like, this area.
Laeticia Matthers:	Is that everything that happened that day?
Marigold Deleanor:	Yes, ma'am. We just kind of left his room after that.
Laeticia Matthers:	And that was the last time?
Marigold Deleanor:	Yeah, that was, like...four or five months ago. He kind of avoided me after that.
Laeticia Matthers:	And then you went to go stay with your grandmother?
Marigold Deleanor:	Yeah, I guess I just felt weird. I don't know. I love my dad. Like, he's a cool guy, like, it's fun to hang out with him, but I don't know...
Laeticia Matthers:	Yes, of course, of course. I understand. Honey, you're totally normal. I talk to people who deal with this all the time. You did nothing wrong. Can you tell me when, approximately, this behaviour started? When he started acting inappropriately?
Marigold Deleanor:	Maybe, like, Grade 6? Like, when we were at the Broadland house.
Laeticia Matthers:	Can you remember any specific behaviour?

Laeticia Matthers: Just, like, touching on me, you know, getting close... There was a time when he got into the shower with me.

Laeticia Matthers: Are you able to describe what happened in the shower?

Marigold Deleanor: Like...he was just naked, like rubbing up against me, from behind, mostly from behind.

Laeticia Matthers: Can you tell me if there was penetration?

Marigold Deleanor: There wasn't, like...not exactly.

Laeticia Matthers: Not exactly?

Marigold Deleanor: I mean, he didn't, but I knew he was there, like...close to me.

Laeticia Matthers: Mm-hmm [affirmative], okay, and this was at Broadland?

Marigold Deleanor: Mm-hmm [affirmative].

Laeticia Matthers: Do you think anyone else in your family was aware of this? This behaviour?

Marigold Deleanor: I don't know. Maybe. My mom always just kind of ignored me. I don't know if she cared. I mean, she probably cared, I don't know, she just didn't know how to act.

Laeticia Matthers: Okay, okay. That's good, you're doing great. Let's focus on your dad

then. What do you think should
happen to him?

Marigold Deleanor: Like...how do you mean?

Laeticia Matthers: Hm, well, you said this has been
going on since you were twelve...

Marigold Deleanor: Around there, I guess. But like, not
all the time. Just sometimes...

Laeticia Matthers: And you're sixteen now. So after
about four years of this ongoing...
situation, do you have a sense of
why you came forward now?

Marigold Deleanor: I guess...like, I didn't really think
about it as bad before? I know that
sounds stupid and, like, dumb or
whatever... It's like, I knew it was
secret, I just...I don't know... And
now it's like, I know.

Laeticia Matthers: Mm-hmm [affirmative], mm-hmm
[affirmative]. What do you know now?

Marigold Deleanor: It's, like, wrong.

Laeticia Matthers: Mm-hmm [affirmative]. And what
do you think should happen to
your dad?

Marigold Deleanor: Like, I know what should happen
but I don't necessarily want it to
happen or...

Laeticia Matthers: What do you think should happen?

Marigold Deleanor: I think he should, like, go to jail...

Laeticia Matthers: Mm-hmm [affirmative], right, right, of course, of course, and-

NEW I hit, NEW I hit, NEW—after six or seven or eight days of refreshing the NEW button and checking, also, that the notifications are in fact turned on, that's all I can find. Blessed to find it. Blessed like I make my own blessings, like I will them into being, like I'm helped by this thing that sits for me, with me, replacing Hank, or else replacing me with everybody augmented, with everybody now held together, or holding, or trying to hold, aligning us to one, eventually. But someone else, somewhere else must have gotten the rest of Marigold's file. Who else is invested? Who else hits NEW, who else has their NOTIFICATIONS turned on for UJANG FEELING? I should start a forum, a fan page, a private chat. Discuss: As suspected, Mona knew; she knew all along. Laeticia hardly offered any support. She just pressed the girl with her saccharine condescension. And I'm wretched. I was waiting for this story, and now that I have it, it's sickening. Sickening even more in its thrill. I'm on edge. I type quickly, I backspace, I make a million mistakes. I listen twice. The girl hardly says anything, I cut out all the "ums." And then I sit alone in my kitchen feeling like I shouldn't know this. I shouldn't know everything about Marigold, the elven waif at the self-checkout counters. I have to do something. Start something. Something, anything, to relieve the feeling of it, the twisting of this fascination, the anger at this repulsion. It's almost as though she's doing it. She's doing this to me.

I know it isn't right, but I blame her. I feel like she owes me something, at least abstractly, obscurely. I feel as though I know her, really know all about her, like I'm in the club, like I'm in the family. And if I was there, I would know the right thing to do, the right thing to say. And if I was there, I would've noticed. Not like Mona—I would've seen. I go back to the grocery store, but the girl is gone.

***

HIT: Determine the Truth of the Following Statement:

CONTEXT: A young woman with a red bikini top is standing with her hands together above her head, while three other people stand directly behind her with their arms in different positions, making the woman in front look as if she has many arms.

STATEMENT: A woman in a green bikini is alone on a beach.

IS THIS STATEMENT TRUE, FALSE, OR NEITHER?

***

Thurston Landover, benevolent businessman, was thought cute and able to alter or upend the streak in Amelia Landover, formerly Callister née LaRoque, that made her naughty. But naughtiness was her character and together they had playful passion, which is what made them, maybe, a favourite on fan forums, along with gutsy Marianna Landover and roguish Cam Jenner. But Marianna and Cam had that soulmate-soft frame. They were always on a wharf, in a cottage, always being kind and supportive and dying over their love for each other. Amelia and Thurston, though, would meet during crisis—in hospital rooms over comatose bodies, in board meetings unexpectedly. Amelia and Thurston would exchange sly looks, look away quickly—they were always on the *precipice of.* Amelia had charm and changeableness, that capricious quality I've read in fan fiction is very beguiling, but the beguiling are prone to evil in daytime TV and the beguiled are set up for heartbreak and a string of crazy ex-lovers who will stop at nothing to retrieve their lost love.

There was a flood of *Bluffs* to be typed out. A few files anyhow, needing my time and attention, needing me to get the names right, needing the transcript turned out on time for whatever purpose, it can only be imagined. I've found archived transcripts on soaponline.pl, on bluff.ru, on various forums, and deposited mysteriously in web directories pointing, apparently, to some insider need for such things. But are they just made to sit, to stay behind, to flood the air and wires and waves with words that were learned and uttered with routine passion? I guess I don't know. I guess I do the files.

Derek DeMarco:	I think it's time you knew the truth.
Thurston Landover:	I don't know who you think you are coming in here like this.
Derek DeMarco:	No one of consequence.
Thurston Landover:	Get out of my house! Who let you in here?
Derek DeMarco:	I'll leave. I'll leave once I've said what I have to say.

Thurston Landover:	This is ridiculous. I'm calling the police.
Derek DeMarco:	They won't help you.
Thurston Landover:	What are you saying? Are you threatening me?
Derek DeMarco:	I know all the cops in this town. Believe me, they won't help you. Besides, what I have to say…you'll want to hear.

I needed to know, but knowing slowed me, saddened me. When I came across Doug's file the first time, I was lit up. I know I was. I wouldn't have told anybody, and, in fact, had I been asked, I would've said the opposite.

Although who would've asked me? I wouldn't have done this sort of work when Margery and Hank were alive. I have this image of my life—though I'm not sure it's how I felt about my life at the time. That thought, singular thought, it's transforming, it's changing, and I don't get to hold on to the way I used to feel. Maybe I don't need to. Maybe those old feelings were ungrateful and small. Maybe I didn't appreciate sitting at the kitchen table—in a clean kitchen, a sparkling kitchen—with Margery while Hank watched fishing shows in the living room, shouting periodically for this sandwich, for that pair of slippers. Always shouting, Hank, a quiet man who rarely shouted, in my mind his plaintive cry has become a gruff and needy shout. Which is true? In which way do I love him more? In which way can I love him at all?

"My God, your sister gossips," I remember saying to him in bed after one of these evenings sitting with Margery and

Mother Penny. We called a taxi for Penny, who was over ninety and had little energy left and ran out of it quickly. Life after fifty, after sixty, after seventy, eighty, ninety—you get more and more tired and just try to maintain, try to keep the edges from fraying off until the inside quits on you, like weeding the garden in November. Penny took a taxi home. And Margery started in on her: "Oh, the old woman, I love her dearly, I do, but my God, when she puts in her two cents, her little *pennies*, where she does, and I just know—I know!—she hasn't a clue what she's talking about. The woman hasn't read a newspaper in forty years but could give you the storyline of six different soap operas like they were world histories! And God knows she doesn't have a computer or any other kind of device. She's got the same TV we bought for her forty years ago—her first TV, would you believe it? A relic, the woman and the set. But I love her, I do, and I know what it's like, of course, getting old, my God, it's always happening, and then it's just already happened. If you've seen Millie Hollit lately—you know, she works at the hardware store—good Lord, good Lord, she looks worked over. I suppose I hadn't been to the hardware store in a while, but Millie, I knew her from school." Margery shouts to the living room, "Hank, you remember Millie Hollit?" No answer. Imperceptibly, or else I imagine it for some petty meanness in my own mind, I think I hear the volume go up—"FIBREGLASS ROD," I'm sure I hear blast from the set.

Margery turns back to me. "We went to school with this woman—she's the same age as Hank and I, Millie is. And yet, you look at her face, she could be a hundred—she could be a hundred! It must be her husband. A real old bastard. He never beat her, nothing like that, but he worked her. You know? He worked the whole family. Seven goddamn children—I think he just had a family to work them. They're basically religious, but their religion is nuts and bolts or something, you know?" She could talk; she could go on.

Hank only laughed when I talked about his sister. I wonder if he knew I loved her, if he knew that this is how sisters talk about sisters. I wonder if he knew how we talked about him. But I don't know what Hank knew, or what Hank cared about, besides fishing. It never showed, or I never bothered looking. When we were one thing, I could hate him and it was no worse than having a mood, my own mood, and a mood passes. But in this pit—all moods are augmented, all moods are reasons and regrets. I did this; I wished this. And now I don't know what I am because I'm no longer me without the cult of us, me and him and his relations—a small but practised gang of habits, a shifting-along organism. Now cut free, I could be anything, but to be anything I would have to want something. In this world in this world.

I used to answer emails at the Park Lodge, years ago—that trailer of an office alongside a third-rate golf course, alongside a sticky clubhouse—and now, halfaman, I start my own email and go forth. And I'm good. I'm a natural. This shiftless dreb has found a thing to do, a thing to be, the eyes, the ears, the fingers. The mind lives elsewhere, all connected, mostly knowing, moods directed to whatever the mind inhabits. Out there, in here. I'm good at this. I was bad at that—I let that stagnate, thinking we could just be still and quiet while time smoothed us out like waves on glass. So, oh well. I'm good at this, and this is what there is now.

***

Okay, I'll live on *The Bluffs*—forget Marigold, forget Hank—
if I can only think endlessly of Christie Callister. The files I
get are random, incomplete, so I fill in the gaps on collective knowledge sites, on forums, through video clips.

Raped, the young girl was raped by a triplet, a secret third
brother, set maliciously upon framing his other brothers for
their privilege. An admitted jealousy undoes him, and he's
nothing underneath. Death, death for the rapist, that's the
soap opera way, lacking the facilities that might offer re-
form. What kind of soap opera would it be if single-minded
villains disappeared for years and came back with coping
strategies and delicate new psyches? "Ted, Tim, I'm your
brother Tom. I know I tried to frame you for the rape of
the beloved Christie Callister for the flimsy reason that you
grew up rich and had every opportunity afforded to you,
and I was raised by a meddling nurse who kidnapped me at
birth and lied about my death, but I'm better now, brothers,
I'm all better."

The three go forth, holding hands, skipping along; they
play in the daisies. Christie comes out and kisses their
heads. "Miss Christie!" they cry—then I cry, then you, the
viewer, cry.

I ate so many fish sandwiches. Hunched over my computer learning about these lives, lying about these lives for
fanfic forums to no acclaim, eating fried fish sandwiches
and leaving wrappers all over the floor. I can smell myself. I can smell my house. We smell different. The house
has an old hot rug smell, like a vacuum that sprays dust
behind as it goes. The house needs an airing; I need to
be wiped down. There's an obsession. I'm living this other
life, listening to it and learning about it. Outside of that,
what is it? That which is not needed has been processed,

and the artifacts lie on my floor, and I am a lumbering ruin in a sea of waxed plastic. There haven't been many files lately besides *The Bluffs*, just bad ones. Things I don't bother with. Heavy static and metallic clinks. Things that scratch at your ears and screech unintelligibly. These robo shrieks, they are not workable.

***

I'll just avoid the Savery. I'll walk as much as I can manage. I'll go to the other grocery stores. The Farmer's on Linkshire, Wilma's on 10th. They hold little interest but neither do they hold guilt or repulsion or obsession—they don't have that. They do have bread and fresher breads, and the difference between the two has appeared to me as apparent, but I've never been tested or tricked by marketing agents either. And they don't have blond girls with long hair and desperate families and scorching glances and lives so different from mine that I sometimes yearn and plead to be as tragic as they are.

Why can't I get used to my own kind of tragedy? Well, maybe that's what I've been doing for the past two or three weeks. Avoiding the Savery, avoiding Marigold, trying to find my own sort of grief as interesting as somebody else's. Is it grief though? It seems to become grief as time goes on. It intensifies or warps, and I sometimes know it's just glass beneath me—not like a stand-in for something but a crunching kind of constant shattering, and if I close my eyes and shake my head, it isn't there, but I know what happens if I open my eyes—a deafening blinding breaking apart that sinks me and I feel everything unlike anything I know—hell. I know what happens if I open my eyes—hell.

I thought it was supposed to get easier. But I guess if you do grief backwards it can only get worse. I faked my tears at Hank's funeral. What a witch. What kind of witch has short grey hair and a pug nose anyway? What kind of witch has little nylon socks always slinking against her ankles and sometimes getting sucked into her shoes? This kind of witch, I answer myself. This kind. Hank's funeral, I went all out, I'll give myself that much. I bought him a sycamore casket. It was fine. Nicer than our bed. Velvet interior, white velvet. I don't think it comes in other colours. Red would be too suggestive, black too morbid, they must think. Maybe purple. Maybe blue. I'm glad I didn't have many to choose from—how are you supposed to think about the colour of the inside of the casket without putting yourself in a casket? What colour should line the eyes of my dead husband for now, forever? Maybe I should've made it simple, given him blue; he was a good boy, a boy who loved fishing, who did his chores—sometimes. He could've had blue, baby blue for baseball and the country sky. But what colour should I get? I don't know if I can think about it. Lying down for that long. Would I—should I—specify somewhere that I want antique hardware on my casket? Would I—should I—specify something about my own me-less future? My will gives nothing to nobody. Not a real anybody. The local thrift store, the library. They'll make me a plaque: "Generous donor: What was her name again?"

So I'm not marching all over the Savery, and I'm not sitting in the small cafeteria next to the self-checkout counters. And I'm not spending much time at the library, not enough that they know me by name, and I'm not spending much time at the ol' Give 'n' Save Thrift. And I'm not really listening to or looking for more dirt on Marigold or anyone else through transcription files—but, well, minor time spent with Christie Callister and city-slicked sleaze (possible love interest?) Eric Emerson. But, well, then what am I doing? Waddling around. Screaming at the pigeons on the roof from my porch. Throwing broken pencils at them. HITs and online surveys for three or thirty cents each.

SURVEY: Read the following statements as they flash on the screen. Do not write them down.

House A has a basement.

House D is in a bad neighbourhood.

House C has a good view.

House A has two bathrooms.

House A has a pool.

House B has no pool.

House D has a good view.

House A is in a suburb.

House A is near a school.

House B has one floor.

House D has no basement.

House C is in a good neighbourhood.

House C is near a park.

House D has a pool.

House B has no basement.

House A is near a park.

House C has two bathrooms.

House D has one bathroom.

House B is in a bad neighbourhood.

House B is near shops and stores.

House A has three levels.

House B has a good view.

House A has a bad view.

House D has two floors.

House C has two bedrooms.

House B has one bathroom.

House C has two floors.

House C has a basement.

ANSWER THE FOLLOWING QUESTIONS USING A SCALE FROM 1 TO 9 WHERE 9 IS VERY LIKELY AND 1 IS NOT LIKELY AT ALL.

1. How likely are you to rent House A?

2. How likely are you to purchase House B?

3. How likely are you to renovate House C?

4. How likely are you to swim in a pool?

5. How likely is it that House D has two bathrooms?

6. How likely is it that House A is destroyed by fire within the next five years?

7. How likely is it that House B will be vandalized?

8. How likely is it that House C will be purchased by a Chinese investor?

9. Select 3 so that we know you are paying attention.

10. How likely is it that House D has a red terracotta roof?

11. How likely are you to live in a house without windows?

IN ONE SENTENCE PLEASE DESCRIBE YOUR CURRENT LIVING CONDITIONS.

My house is my body.

THANK YOU FOR PARTICIPATING. PLEASE DO NOT PARTICIPATE AGAIN.

***

I don't even need anything at the grocery store. And I may have lost interest in savings. Why did I go so often anyway? I don't think I always did. Well, that's not true. We bought fresh food for dinner. We didn't hoard it up. But I used to just stop in, stop for a quick pickup. I didn't often linger the way I've lately taken to lingering. I suppose when I lingered, Hank asked what I was doing—when he was there. Or he asked where I'd been—when he was home. Either way, I was accountable. It's a terrible freedom to linger unaccounted for. I could buy something or nothing. I could stockpile bagged salad and throw it all out if I wanted. Maybe that's an antisocial gesture. I didn't do it; I didn't stockpile greens. Though I entertained the idea. I entertain a lot of ideas while I wander the aisles. I've taken to the ethnic food aisles lately as well. Well, not quite lately but nearly lately. Lately as in after Hank died and before I grew tired of wandering the aisles. There was an in-between time in which I found some joy in bulk cumin powder. Hank, of course, hated spice. I never blasted his dinner, but sometimes I'd throw a jalapeno in the boxed taco mix and search his face to see if he noticed. You couldn't even taste it. It was one little pepper cooked into dust and he'd hoot and "woooooo" and I'd tell him, "Don't be silly." But it was selfish of me to flavour my food. Suffer on salt. I knew how to feed Hank, and I should've stuck to feeding him. Wandering the aisles as though anything goes. I'm eating shredded pork from a plastic bin, lychee in syrup, supremely spiced sauces all over my bologna. But I miss tacos, plain old boxed tacos and salt-seasoned meat. But even when I go back to that, even when I return to a shaked-up baked-up pork chop, I can't rekindle my interest. Like leaving the past and growing tired of the future and finding them both out of reach. "Obviously," Hank would've said, "obviously."

***

To try to enjoy the peace I thought I wanted—and must endure all the more bitterly for having entertained the want—I'll take up my terrible freedom: I'll go for an aimless walk. Lump my thick stumps down, one after the other; I don't need a purpose, don't need groceries, don't need Quickburger. I'll walk around and look at the town in which I live and the town in which I've worked and the town in which I've retired. This is my town, but do I know it? I'll walk it. This is my mission, and I walk with a new purpose of no purpose. Or maybe there can't be nothing, so one must endure the invented something, and this purpose made now was to *know*. To see the town I thought I knew. To re-see. To find beauty. To walk and breathe and make a commercial of the old girl feeling hope, renewal, the joy before the disclaimer.

Though it's a short-lived resolution, or else it's replaced by another resolution following a brief spell of repulsion after an incident with a family at the library loading dock.

It's a young family, and they're gathered up together behind the library, standing with anxious impermanence near the cement loading dock's short wall. The mother is young, no older than eighteen; her skin looks scratched. In one arm, she awkwardly holds an oversized child bundled in unseasonal snow gear, and in her other hand, a filled-up, beat-up stroller. The child in the stroller screams insanely and spits forth foam and shrill desperation. A third child stands—the eldest, it seems—alongside the stroller shouting in short angry bursts, "SH! SH! SH!" The shushing elder rests a filthy mitten in the hand of their father, who himself looks like an old, insipid teen. He's gangly and his clothes are purposeful rags. His one hand is occupied by the eldest child, his other attempting to light a child-sized bong resting on the lap of the toddler in the stroller. The bong is of an absurd size to have outside of the house, let alone have placed on a child's lap while stationed beside a library loading dock. I walk past, and if I was farther away, I might've found some fascination in the spectacle of them, but I'm too close; there's a risk of absorption. I can smell the lot of them. Not just the drugs, but the Froot Loops on the child's breath, the sweat-muddled fabric of the mother's acrylic knit cardigan, the father's shit-smeared shoe. I retreat, terrified that I might be sucked in, forced to endure something fetid, moist, and seeping. I walk quickly past and resolve that when I get home, I'll clean my house, I'll clean my kitchen.

Fate, though, steps in and delays me. Sure. One can't clean a kitchen quickly when fate steps in. Certainly. I walk with determination. Or I try. Unsightly, my heavy waddle—probably, maybe to me, who knows how it looks to them, like I say, I don't think about it, no, I don't like to think about it. I think about this: I'm stuffing the trash bags in my mind with waxy paper wrappers. I hardly notice at all when I bump into little Marigold. She looks so small on the street. A breeze. "Excuse me!" I'm profuse.

"Don't worry about it," she says sadly, without looking up, and walks on.

I'm rerouted though, still with my determined energy, and now the thrill of another episode. Cliffhanged and hooked. "How's your grandmother?" I shout in an unfamiliar voice.

She turns. "My grandmother?" she asks slowly, confused.

"Yes, sorry, I'm Norma." I stick out my hand. "I think I know your grandmother from city council meetings. Oh, I haven't been to a meeting in months, but I'm sure I saw her there when I used to go."

"I don't think so." Marigold's room-temperature hand sits in my clammy meathook for almost a second before she pulls it away and looks relieved that it's been a mistake, that I'm mistaken. I don't know her; I don't know her grandmother. And if I let it go, I'm sure everything will settle neatly.

"Rosa Deleanor?" I name the woman. I name her! As though we were intimate, as though we'd had brunch and tea and played cards together.

"Yeah…"

"I thought so." At least I'm unfamiliar to myself. At least this shouting woman staring deeply and intently into a poor child's eyes isn't the pathetic hunched widow I'd dragged toward the library loading dock. "Well, darling, I hope she's well. You can tell her Norma says hello."

"Okay," Marigold says sadly, baffled.

"Listen, hon, are you all right?"

"It's...nothing. It's really nothing."

And this is when I really go crazy. The determined version bursts forth, pulling honeys, sweeties, bootstraps, and hair. Maybe I invoke Margery. Maybe I invoke the old lady I think I look like when I brush my teeth. *SEE ME*. I know I'm old and worn in. I know from the look of me what I should be, and by now I should've figured out how to pull it off. I should pat waitresses on the hand and call them "dear," I should complain about my meal without shame, I should send back the curdled milk rather than drinking it, squinching. So here I am, emerged on the street. "Listen, doll, have you got a pen?"

"I guess so." Marigold searches her purse for a pen and hands it to me.

"And a piece of paper." I laugh, like a real loud comforting obnoxious laugh. A strange laugh that makes other people feel small but okay because it takes all the pressure off them and puts all the pressure on me to hold the conversation and direct the conversation and start and end and slightly condescend.

"Sure," Marigold says without real commitment to her movements, with light fluid gestures; she hands me the paper and looks briefly into my eyes, searching for something, maybe recognition, or else a friend. We knew each other then. For a second. She must see that I'm not a loud woman making demands on the sidewalk. She must see my dirty kitchen and doesn't mind, knows my mind. And this girl, she's alone. I see it in her wispy fingers.

"Listen, honey, here's my address. I live right around the corner. Come by if you ever need to talk. I know your grandma, lovely woman. You know, I must've met you before too. Maybe you were around one day while we were playing cards. You look familiar to me. Listen, come by...or here, I'll write my number down—give me a call. I can help. I can help you. You can talk to me if you need to." My heart beats loudly. I'm not coming up with the right words, the right arrangement. I have her for an instant, I've hypnotized her, she's looking at me, handing me pens and papers, and imagining me playing cards with her grandmother, and then an unravelled end. My words are insistent but missing that disposable breeze that would've made them real. Can you fake that? Vivienne LaRoque could. I smile and turn to leave quick before anything else can fall off me. I just have to move away without tripping or spitting or ripping my dress. I don't even look at her as I leave. I just say, with meaningful pauses, "If you ever need anything..." Which is really good, I think, my tone is perfect, off-handed, and if the rest of my talk had been more precise, if I'd been more convincing, it would've been the perfect exit. As it is, I think I've only succeeded in neutralizing my overall effect. And maybe that's enough.

***

What is this—old woman? I used to be reasonable. That life with Hank. We did so little and felt so little, and that was nice, it was. We were so regular. He worked for most of our lives. He drove a forklift, he packed boxes, he moved to an office, he supervised forklift drivers, he ordered boxes. I worked for most of our lives, mainly admin; I answered phones, learned the books. And then we retired. It was nice—why would I tell myself it wasn't nice? Who was I when I was with him and his mother and his sister and we made a turkey and the potatoes came out gummy? Why couldn't I see that that was the best of me? There was laughter among us, and what else could I hope for? "Darling, these potatoes are fucking terrible." Hank, you old bastard, I know, don't you think I know that? I should've laughed, but I soured and flung my head back. Today I laugh! Today, when it doesn't matter, I want to work it all out. I can't even regret properly; this isn't regret over failed ambition, it's regret over my failure to see love when I had it. What am I missing right now? That's exactly the problem: my love, myself, old Norma, there's nothing here to miss; it's only over there to miss, in the past, irretrievable. *Fuck me*. Hank would've laughed at that.

I'll calm down and remember. I will. I'll remember how he annoyed me. "Fucking Norma, woman, you leave the cupboards open, you leave the lights on, what're you about?"

"What am I about, you bastard, what am I about? I'm about sixty-five years old, and if I leave the cupboards open, I leave the goddamn cupboards open," I said while walking through the kitchen, slamming cupboard doors.

"Yeesh."

"Let's not bicker, old man; it's tiresome." I dismissed him back to the living room; he sighed but didn't say anything.

And what I didn't say, what I never thought, is what the alternative could've been. What the sprawling aimless alternative could've been. Oh me oh me oh me—

This will pass, of course. I've met a celebrity on the street and I've come undone. It's nerves, the nerves, nothing calming my nerves.

HIT: What do you think of these brand names?

YEEM
URB

1. WHICH DO YOU PREFER?

Urb.

2. WHY DO YOU PREFER IT?

For the love of U.

3. ARE YOU LIKELY TO PURCHASE PRODUCTS FROM THE BRAND NAME YOU SELECTED?

What does Urb sell? Well, it's for me to decide, here, in my kitchen, on my home computer, and then tell the survey and the collector of data, the compu-collector, why it is I want Urb over Yeeb and the products within. Who is this Urb dweller who wonders after me and sees me, my clacks and bits, as a contribution? It's always a guy named Elvis in a lab coat— how can I help what we see?

No. I am not likely to.

4. THANK YOU FOR PARTICIPATING IN OUR SURVEY. PLEASE DO NOT PARTICIPATE AGAIN.

***

My house is clean; it's panic clean. It's running-around-the-block clean. I've done it; I've made the floors sparkle and gleam, and I've never felt better about linoleum. I'm ready, should the girl stop by, should the girl come over. What a responsible old lady I'll seem. Maybe I'll put on some lipstick and pull out a tumbler. She'll say, "Here's a sassy old broad I could see myself becoming. Look at the fun-loving whimsy of this kook; what a lively spirit the old witch has." She'll imagine her old age as mine. I'll be enviable.

"Do you live here alone?" she'll ask.

"I do, I do. The old boy died months ago," I'll cackle, then throw down a beer and light a joint that hangs from the end of a long holder. She can't get a handle on me. I'm elusive; I'm useful.

"I just feel stupid, you know? Like I just should've known better, known what to do... Something in me liked being seen, and then, and then that feeling became different—I don't know, it transformed... I just feel so stupid now, disgusting, embarrassed. I'm ashamed, I guess," she'd tell me, and I'd look at her through the smoke with this half-cocked air, like I was gonna offer advice and this was the moment she was waiting for. I had it, I'd seen it all.

"Honey," I'd tell her, "you didn't do nothing wrong. You're such a pretty young thing—" No, I couldn't say that. That would be weird; that isn't the right thing. "Honey, you can't help how you feel—" It's flat, it's fucking flat! Which me, where am I—okay, okay, Norma clears the air, Norma makes it right. "Honey, there's nothing you can do about what he did." Sure, okay, that could be it. Is that it? Does that mean enough? We'll find out when she gets here, when she comes over, when she sees me and includes me and needs me. I get called back for a second episode. A second season. I'm a major character.

Bob Fielder: ...tips to help you get through tax time on WXNP News at six.

Dana Cardiff: Here it comes, television's most exciting hour of fantastic prizes on *Spin to Win!*

Announcer 1: Hello, everybody. Hello. Welcome to *Spin to Win*, television's most exciting game show. We have our two contestants right here, Dana Cardiff and Scott McPherson. Dana, why don't you tell us a little bit about yourself.

Announcer 2: Well, okay, yes, Bob. I'm a schoolteacher from Indiana, and I'm married with three children. Sheila, Mindy, and David is the youngest. My husband, Dan, just loves you, Bob. He loves you, and he loves this show, and I'm just so happy to be here.

Bob Fielder: Okay, Dana, all right, good stuff, Dana. And what grade do you teach in Indiana, Dana?

Dana Cardiff: I teach fourth grade, Bob.

Bob Fielder: Fourth grade? Well, that's not so bad, that's not so bad. I'm sure your students are excited to see you on TV and they're all glued to their seats watching you.

Dana Cardiff: Oh yes, Bob.

Bob Fielder:	All right, very good. Good luck to you, Dana, and tell Dan I love him too. All right, all right, Scott, can you tell us what you do and where you're from?
Scott McPherson:	Well, Bob, I have a bit of an unusual job. I work for myself, Bob, and I spend a lot of time on the beach.
Bob Fielder:	Gee, Scott, that doesn't sound too bad.
Scott McPherson:	Not at all, Bob. I'm a treasure hunter. I use a metal detector to find precious items. That's what I do for a living, Bob.
Bob Fielder:	Like a scavenger, you might say.
Scott McPherson:	Well, no, Bob, I wouldn't say that. I consider myself a treasure hunter, and I love what I do. I'm from a little place in California called Redondo Beach. Well, not too little, Bob.
Bob Fielder:	That's great, that's just great, Scott. And can you tell us what the most valuable thing you've ever found is?
Scott McPherson:	Sure, Bob. I once found a gold nugget buried deep in the sand, like a pirate's treasure. Someone must have buried it there, because gold like that isn't normally found on the beach. This gold nugget weighed almost two pounds, and it's the most valuable thing I've found to date.

Bob Fielder: That is some nugget, Scott. You didn't bring it with you today, did you, Scott?

Scott McPherson: No, I didn't, Bob.

Bob Fielder: Oh, okay. I thought maybe you brought it for luck. He didn't bring it. Well, he didn't bring it. That's all right, that's okay. We've got enough luck for everybody. We certainly do. And when we come back, we'll put that luck to the test.

Bob Fielder: Norma Nimmo, tell us about yourself.

Norma looks around; I look around. I see me, and I am what I see. The stage is flashy and located off the living room. The back of Hank's head mountains up from the horizon of the scratchy plaid chair. I walk to him knowing he'll be limp. Bob Fielder is standing at the self-checkout counter next to the television talking to Marigold. They're both eyeballing me. Hank smiles an old smile, a smile I haven't seen in thirty years. He's alive. He loves me. I flush. I'm twenty-two years old, but I'm small like a child looking up at him. "Hank? This is a dream. I know it's a dream."

"So what?" he says, and laughs, and I'm reminded of his mild humour and slow nature before he grew tired and used to me, before I grew tired and used to him. I laugh too, and I sit on his lap. He's warm, and I can smell the dust in the chair. I spend too long smelling the chair, and his heavy arms melt; the chair is a cart driving through the grocery store. Bob Fielder is running after me telling me I haven't won anything. "You still have to spin!" he shams to an audience while becoming winded and masking it poorly.

"I'm killing him," I say and stop my cart. I try to comfort Bob Fielder, to hold him up. I'm sure he's dying; he's dying because he was chasing me, because I was running from him, and so I try to help, to hold him up. He's heavy, much heavier than he looks; he's heavy like Hank was heavy when I found him fallen half out of his chair and I tried to push him back, to sit him up, to make him look like he was asleep, just watching TV. Bob is Hank, and he's smiling again. I let us fall, and the ground gives way. We're falling, and the floor is water. I'm alone now, and I can breathe in liquid. But I'm alone. It's dark and everything light is left above. I turn toward the surface and see Marigold pointing down at me, and Bob Fielder whispering to a heavy-set police officer with a notepad—I swim quickly away. I awake in a fright that fades beneath Hank's arms around me. I feel the familiar skin of them, the sweat of them, the weight of them. I'm warm from the sun through the gauzy white curtains. I reach my arm slowly around his thick waist and breathe deep. I feel his wrinkled neck at my nose, then my forehead. My heart is tight in my chest; my eyes are hot with tears. I keep them closed, tightly closed. It doesn't matter what they want from me. It doesn't matter what anybody wants. My eyes fight the fade of his arms in the rising sun.

***

I get up slowly, begging my body to relapse, to collapse again into the lying dream. I look at myself in the bathroom mirror. I look tired. I have two thick pouches beneath my eyes, delicate but persistent. I don't know what they do. It seems there should be less and less of me until one day I shrink or crumple and there's no face left to wash, just a snap, a pop, the slow circulating air rearranging the dust on the rose-coloured sink of a blush-coloured bathroom. But instead I feel as though I gather weight and pox and pouches and carry puckered meat upon bones increasingly unable to bear the load. The pouches are yellowish with lines of blue. My skin is dry with rough patches, and for a moment I consider not washing my face or brushing my teeth.

I was never the kind of person to question the distinct duties that make up each day and must be renewed as often. I've generally enjoyed the fuss. I like to wipe down the counter. I like to dry my body with a clean towel. I like to empty the trash can and rinse it out on the sidewalk with the hose, then rinse the sidewalk off and send the dust and dirt into the gutter. But this day, and, lately, these days, I feel like I can't wash the sleep from my eyes or wash, let alone dry, my tired patchy face.

I'm looking at me but I'm not looking—there's a woozy elsewhere like a car alarm distracting me from some music playing, and I have to think to try to hear, but when the alarm stops, there's nothing else. No sound. Tactile silence. My eyes are swimming, and my body is reaching blindly—a dizzying ache with no fine location. The longer I look, the farther my eyes swim and the stiffer my body grows in its overextension.

I remember, though, that I've given the girl from the grocery store my address and phone number, and, rather than dwelling on why she might not come and what she might've thought of the Norma she met in the street, I consider that if she does come, perhaps on her way to work, unable to bear the load, like me, but her, with her thoughts, she'll stop in and say, "I thought you might want to have a cup of tea." I'll fix it for her, and the house will fill with use and warmth and the sound of a screaming kettle. So I brush my teeth and clean afterwards the splattered mirror and feel a rush of movement from movement and dry my face and make my bed and put on a dress. After breakfast I'll do the shopping, I'll take a walk around the town, I'll work, perhaps—maybe I'll get a job outside the house. All this sitting and looking can't be good for me, for my old back or my veined legs. I have something to squeeze out of the old beanbag yet.

∗∗∗

HIT: Determine the Truth of the Following Statement:

CONTEXT: A bluebird lands on the edge of a bird bath made of white marble.

STATEMENT: A bad bird has bitten a boy.

IS THIS STATEMENT TRUE, FALSE, OR NEITHER?

Perhaps, I think, it was the boy who was bad and not the bird, thus rendering the statement FALSE and even more so FALSE than I had imagined it could be because the boy was never bitten at all. Perhaps—I think in images—the boy came later and smashed the bath and made off with the statue—a lovely little winged Nike—and the bird. But this is a bird in name only, conjured easily by that name—wearing blue like a coat draped over an idea at any moment prone to dissipation by the upheaval of the coat—what was beneath, where was the bird? He-bird wriggled free and went after the boy, bit the boy, snapped at the boy, laid beak upon the boy, and flew toward freedom with Nike in tow. But of course the statement is FALSE simply because there is no boy and there is no bite. The bird cannot bite even if there were a bite or there were a boy. A bird can snap and claw, but can a bird bite? Teeth-free, the winged thing pecks helplessly at the empty viciousness of a thieving child. And so I must choose NEITHER, for who knows what happens next in the consequence of things. No, of course they desire FALSE for their answer or else they would've mentioned the boy initially, and the marble is only mentioned—not as a conjurer of precious things or refinement, of hope for peaceful coexistence among man, bird, beast, and beauty—to distract, to suggest that there's more, and more exists outside the image, but if it's more unstated, then it isn't more at all. There's nothing outside the picture. Report only on the picture. Take your two pennies and leave.

***

Robot: Welcome to Quickburger. What can I get for you?

Customer: Four-piece nugget meal.

Robot: Okay.

Customer: Put the cola with it.

Robot: Okay.

Customer: I want a ice cream.

Robot: Okay.

Customer: That's it.

Robot: Would you like anything else?

Customer: No.

Robot: If everything looks correct on the screen, your total will be $11.54. Please drive to the first window.

Customer: Okay.

Thus they did converse.

***

I've got my lipstick on. A nice soft pearly puce. I've got my shoes on, little brown wedges, comfy wedges. I've got my nylons on and my red polka-dot dress. I put mascara on my eyes; I've slapped my cheeks and made them rosy. I'm ready to go. I'm ready to go out. To do my errands. Pick up my groceries. Make a nice dinner. Eat it alone on the porch, looking into the sun and letting my eyes go blind and burnt. I'm ready to finish dinner and eat a pie, a whole pie—gooseberry, strawberry, Saskatoon berry, raspberry pie, blackberry pie. I'm here ready to eat a grape-filled pie, a raisin crumble. Hank always wanted apple. I'm sitting here ready to fix, to keep fixing. It takes doing: you do and you keep doing. You don't stop moving. I'm here ready to beat the rugs and sweep the floor. I'm here ready to clear out the basement. I'm sitting here in my raincoat ready to check the mail and pay the bills. I'm sitting here. I'm sitting here.

***

Tim Kinder: Listen to me, Christie. It wasn't me. You know it wasn't. I was with your own brother the night you claim-

Christie Callister: I claim! The night I claim it happened. That's real rich, coming from you. My brother said they paged you over and over, and when you finally got to the operating room you were out of breath. Andrea could have died. What exactly were you doing?

Tim Kinder: Don't be ridiculous. Are you actually trying to convince yourself that I somehow assaulted you and operated on Andrea Wesley at the same time? Or are you saying I raced to the hospital after raping you?

Christie Callister: Well, it wasn't Ted. We know that now. We have footage of him from the hospital parking lot. Footage you're mysteriously missing from.

Tim Kinder: Christie! I came in the back entrance, through the laundry room. We've been over this! Again and again! We've been over this.

Christie Callister: Tim, I know what happened to me. And I know what I saw. There's nothing else to explain it. You raped me, Tim. And I'm pressing charges.

***

Amelia Landover:	Thurston, you have to believe me. The man is insane! I've never seen him before in my life.
Thurston Landover:	He has pictures, Amelia. Pictures of the two of you together.
Amelia Landover:	So he had them made. Don't believe him. You can't believe him. He's the man who kidnapped our child-
Thurston Landover:	I don't even know if Jason is my child...
Amelia Landover:	Of course Jason is your child! The DNA test proved that. Derek DeMarco is nothing but a two-bit con man. I don't know what he's after, but I bet it's got a number attached.
Thurston Landover:	Amelia, I want to believe you, I do. But...
Amelia Landover:	Then believe me. Believe me because you love me, and believe me because I'm telling the truth. I wouldn't lie to you, Thurston.

*** * ***

Derek DeMarco:	When Thurston sees this tape of Amelia switching the results of the DNA test, he'll leave her. Amelia will have no choice but to come clean and come back to me.

***

By the time I leave my house, it's dark and my lipstick is smudged. I don't know it's smudged until I see my reflection in a window in the milk aisle. I rub the smear from my mouth with the inside of my coat sleeve. I smooth down my hair. I shuffle a little. I know I do; I can feel the shuffle against the scuffed beige floor, but still I shuffle. I'm beginning to wonder if all this mooning about town doesn't have some performative aspect. I've wondered what it would be like to be seen, but I haven't done anything to be praised for and so I shuffle to make a scene. And yet, would I not shuffle if I were alone in the world? Being alone in the world, I confirm that I would shuffle because I do shuffle. I wonder, though, if I were alone in the world, would I wipe the lipstick from my mouth? And determine that no, I would spread it further. I kiss the glass in the frozen pizza aisle and leave a small smudge. "Hi, Mari," I say to the girl by the counter.

"Marigold..." she says as I talk and talk and try to figure out how to set fire to a wet log. A log that needs to be lit. It's cold, and the only way to cook this frozen pizza is over an outdoor fire, but it's been raining and there's little chance the log will light. If perhaps someone would find some kindling, we could move this thing along, but me, I'll just keep at it, hunched over the log. Ow, my thumb is numb from flicking the lighter.

"I just hope you're doing all right. I really do. You're such a nice girl. I know; I come here. I'm friends with your grandmother, that's right, we met at church, I think. No, rather it was at a town hall meeting. A couple of times I'm sure we've played cards. Rosa, lovely woman. It's too bad about her son. Your father, it seems. How is Doug? Won't you tell me how Doug is? No, never mind, we don't have to go into it here, just tell me you're doing all right. I know you are, of course you are, you're a sweet girl. Really, dear, you should look into modelling. See these magazines? Over here, this rack? It's a large rack with a lot to choose from, I could see you there, your face spread across the cover. Well, darling, just getting myself a frozen pizza, just thought I'd pick up something to eat, I do love pepperoni... Oh, but this is a veggie option, you know I wasn't looking, go figure, silly me, I just grabbed any old pizza, how about I just eat a veggie pizza! What would Hank say? Goodness, goodness, send my regards, darling, tell your grandmother I say hello. Please tell her."

Does the girl shudder? I can only tell you about the infinitely small caving of her chest, the slightest lift of her shoulders, the gentlest tilt of her chin. But I'm moving too quickly to rely on my own observations. I'm moving quickly. I'm grabbing a frozen pizza and stuffing it under my arm, cold up against my armpit; I'm walking out the door; I'm picking up an application form from the customer service table; I'm making my way home.

***

SURVEY: Read the following paragraph and answer the questions that follow:

Gemma works as a secretary in a law firm. She is very beautiful, but she doesn't know it. She dresses in cheap clothes that don't fit her very well. One day she is called into her boss's office. Her boss is Rich Redling, a tall handsome man with an air of mystery. He invites Gemma to dine with him. Gemma is flattered, and although she isn't sure if it's appropriate to go out on a date with her employer, she accepts the invitation. When Gemma leaves his office, she is blushing. Deborah, one of the paralegals, approaches Gemma and tells her to beware of Rich. Deborah tells Gemma that Rich is trying to take advantage of Gemma's naïveté. Gemma tells Deborah that she can take care of herself. Later that evening, while Gemma is preparing for her date, there is a knock at the door. Rich has sent over a beautiful golden gown for Gemma to wear. There's a note: "Put this on and meet me on the roof." Gemma obeys.

ON A SCALE OF 1 TO 6, 6 BEING STRONGLY DIS-AGREE AND 1 BEING STRONGLY AGREE, RESPOND TO THE FOLLOWING STATEMENTS:

1. Gemma reminds me of myself.

2. Gemma reminds me of someone I know.

3. Rich reminds me of someone I know.

4. Deborah reminds me of someone I know.

5. I am like Deborah.

6. I would meet Rich on the roof.

7. I would take Deborah's advice.

8. I trust Rich.

9. I trust Deborah.

10. I am unlike Gemma.

ANSWER THE FOLLOWING QUESTIONS BRIEFLY:

1. What do you think will happen to Gemma on the roof?

2. Do you think Deborah cares about what happens to Gemma?

3. How can you relate Gemma's experience to your own life?

4. How can you relate Rich's experience to your own life?

5. Are you interested in working for a law firm?

6. Are you interested in wearing a golden gown?

7. How many costume balls have you attended?

8. How many tuxedos do you think the average man owns?

9. Do you want Gemma to get married?

10. How would Gemma's marriage impact your life?

THANK YOU FOR PARTICIPATING. YOU WILL NOT RECEIVE A REWARD FOR PARTICIPATING AGAIN.

What will I receive? Is this my content if I type it out for you— you who doesn't yet know what to do with me?

***

Robot: Welcome to Quickburger. What can I get for you?

Customer: Ice.

Robot: Okay. What would you like to drink?

Customer: Milk.

Robot: This customization is not available.

Customer: Water.

Robot: Okay. What else would you like?

Customer: [inaudible]

Robot: I do not understand.

Customer: Give me a sandwich.

Robot: Okay. What kind of sandwich would you like?

Customer: Bacon.

Robot: Okay. Would you like anything else?

Customer: I don't want that.

Robot: Okay. Would you like anything else?

Customer: Just ice.

Robot: Okay. If everything looks correct on the screen, your total will be twenty-five cents. Please drive to the first window.

Customer: I'm not paying that. What is that? What is that?

Robot: I'm sorry. I do not understand.

Customer: What am I paying twenty-five cents for?

Robot: If everything is correct on the screen, your total will be twenty-five cents.

***

HIT: Determine the Truth of the Following Statement:

CONTEXT: Three people lead three horses across the plains.

STATEMENT: A horse can outlive a man.

IS THIS STATEMENT TRUE, FALSE, OR NEITHER?

NEITHER
DO I CARE FOR GEMMA
NOR AM I READY FOR MY FISH FILET
I WON'T WONDER WHAT MY LIFE IS LIKE IF
I'M NOT WALKING ACROSS THE DESERT
ACROSS THE PLAINS
IF I'M NOT BALANCING IN THE CENTRE OF A
SPINNING WHEEL
IF I CAN EXPECT DEBORAH TO COME TO THE
WEDDING AND WORSHIP AT MY FEET AND FUCK
RICH REDLING IN THE CLOAKROOM
AND WHAT ABOUT WE WALK OUT ON THE PLAINS
AND LET THE IMAGES FADE AWAY AND LET THE
OTHERS GO RUNNING FREE LIKE ANCIENT HORSES
OUTLIVING MEN OUTLIVING MEN ALL WE DO IS
WORSHIP GIVE UP ON US
TRUE
FALSE
NEITHER

***

Manager: Hi, Norma, Ms. Nimmo… Can I call you
                Norma?

Norma Nimmo: Missus, sorry, Miss, yes... Call me Norma.

Manager: And, Norma, do you mind if we record you here today? It's part of our interview process. It's confidential, only management and the transcriptionist will hear it.

Norma Nimmo: Mind? I don't mind, sure I don't mind-

Manager: Great. Norma, I see you wrote "floral department" on your application. Can you tell me why you'd like to work in the floral department?

Norma Nimmo: It seems nice. I think it just seems nice. I've seen the people here, I've been coming here for years, since, well, since long before my husband, Hank, died, since we moved into the house on Cedar Street, you know Cedar Street? Right, sure, just around the corner, that must have been thirty-three years ago. I probably know your dad, did your dad run this store? Is this a family business? Sorry, I don't want to talk about that if you don't want to talk about that. I've been coming here since we left that house on Princess and moved to the house on Cedar; we were only on Cedar...oh, sorry, Princess, I mean...for eight or nine years. Hank hated it, the neighbours there were nosy, always peering in. He just liked to be left alone, I guess. I got like that too, I guess. I just liked to be alone with him, but I didn't really. I just accepted it, but also I did love his family, and the house on Princess was farther from Margery, that was his sister. She died too, her death was ugly, bloated and ugly, but you don't want to talk about that, oh my, oh... Sorry, you wanted to know... I'm just running off at the mouth, can't say I've really spoken to anyone since Hank died...well, that's not true of course. There were the people at the funeral home, there was old Lloyd who came out to the ceremony, a couple of folks from the factory, Ted, Tim, the Kinders there, and that sweet girl at the self-checkout counters, she visits me, well, she hasn't yet, but you know, I know all about her, and I really think I could be of use, I could help her. Sorry, look at me, running off at the mouth. I could help you, I mean...I'm a gardener. I have plants on the mantle, I have a rose bush in the front yard. The yard is looking worse for wear since Hank died...no, before, well, worse now, but anyway, I'm ready to start, to start over, to begin, to really begin. I think I mentioned that, oh, but look at me, look at me...

Manager: Okay, Norma, that sounds good. I'm sorry to hear about your husband. If you don't mind, we don't have a lot of time here today... Maybe just tell me why you're looking to get back into the workforce.

Norma Nimmo: Back in, back in, sure. I've only been out for three years or so, I only just retired. I was a secretary and bookkeeper for many years, many, many years. I worked for...you know the Regency Steak House? Corporate headquarters. Worked there for almost twenty years, and after that, I went to the Wharf, out on the water, you know the place. They closed though. After that I answered the phones and did the emails for the Park Lodge out at the golf course. Then I retired, oh you know, I retired. I retired and Hank died. He was older, a bit older, a few years anyway, and he died, but I had already retired, that isn't his fault. It isn't his fault. I retired, and he died, one has nothing to do with the other. Time is brain. I retired. I am retired. I'd like to work here. I come here already. I can be of use. I don't need to do the books. Just something nice. It's nice here. I come here already. I come and I talk to Marigold at the self-checkout, I know Doris from the customer service counter. It's nice here. I come here already.

Manager: Norma, you know, I really appreciate you coming in today. I do appreciate that. Norma, I want you to stop by the customer service counter on your way out and we'll give you a gift certificate for fifteen dollars. I know you come here, Norma, and we appreciate it. I'm not sure we're hiring in the floral department right now, but we'll let you know when we are. Thanks again, Norma.

Norma Nimmo: I'm not crazy.

Manager: No, Norma, I didn't think you were. You take care, Norma. Thank you so much for coming in.

***

I'm just arranging the flowers; I'll show them I can do it. I'll pick up my gift certificate after, on the way out. It's nice, nice of them to offer me that, to let me have that. And I'll just show them I'm ready to work. I know I talk; I talk sometimes. People talk, but I'm ready to work, I'm ready to work. It'll be good for me. I straighten the plant pots a bit, make sure they're all in a neat row. I arrange a little bouquet; I match the dyed daisies with the white carnations. The middle-aged woman with thick glasses I've seen in this section sometimes, I don't see her now. They need someone who cares. I could care. And the daisies look nice with the carnations, all arranged the way I arrange them. I just pick up things as I see them. There's a receipt on the floor by checkout three; I put it in my pocket because no one has shown me where the trash can is—all in good time. I can just help. Like I told the young man, I come here already. I know everyone already. And Marigold standing there at the end of the self-checkout looking a little forlorn is probably thinking, *Where's Doris?* or probably hoping for someone better, more useful, more able to relate to this feeling, whatever the feeling is. Doris has never suffered; what does Doris know about life? Here comes the real Doris.

"Marigold, Marigold, I think I should talk to your father. I can help." Now the professional.

"Help what? What are you talking about?"

"You know—" I give her a sympathetic but confidential look "—we don't have to go into it. But I get it. Let's just say I get it. I understand, Marigold. And your father, he's not a bad guy—well, he is and he isn't. But he's... In spite of what he's done, I know you still love him. I hope you don't mind if I speak openly." Not Doris. I don't know this character; I must've pulled up the stock figure of a doctor, of a psychiatrist, of the Laeticia Matthers I knew I could be. Where was she during the interview? Marigold though seems panicked, breathes quickly, her little face twists painfully. "Are you all right, dear?" I reach out, touch her shoulder; it's small, and immediately I see a bird.

"Who are you?" she demands. "Who are you?!" she bellows, backing into the centre of the six self-checkout stands, three facing three, one of which is occupied by a man in a black baseball hat who cannot be deterred from buying a variety pack of Gatorade.

"Mari, Marigold, I'm Norma. Norma Nimmo. Ms. Nimmo. Nimmo. Nimmo. I hope you're feeling all right. We've met a few times. I used to play cards with your grandmother, Rosa." I maintain my calm; I'm perfectly cast.

I'm no longer babbling obscenely. I'm in complete control. Marigold moves away though. She starts screaming, screaming like some dark figure has risen from the corner and no matter how much she refocuses her eyes, blinking and squinting, rubbing them and pressing her temples, the figure only grows more terrifying, more strange, and it moves with ever-growing urgency, near her, toward her, upon her. But the figure isn't me; I know she's mistaken something. I'm caring; I'm in the role of caregiver. Maybe she doesn't know that; maybe she hasn't figured it out.

Doris comes from nowhere, pulls my shoulders, and frowns. "Ma'am," she says, "I'm sorry, I'm not sure what's going on here, but I really think it's best if you leave the store." Marigold's being pulled away by a woman from the meat department. They move quickly, hunched and gathered.

"Oh, this has been a mistake," I tell Doris. "I know Marigold. She didn't realize maybe, but we've met several times. I know the family. Doris, though, you should check on her. I think something has upset her, and I know what good care you take of her."

"Ma'am, do I know you?" Doris looks perturbed. Annoyed! No one is acting right. "I'm Norma," I tell her. "I'm new."

"Norma, okay, it's been very nice to meet you," she says slowly, leading me toward the door, "but I think it's best if you don't come back for a while. Just for a while, Norma. Maybe something has upset—" she hesitates, as though she doesn't want to say her name "—Marigold. And I just think it's best if we give her some time and space."

"Tell her to come see me," I say to Doris. "Tell her I have different kinds of tea."

***

I sit in Hank's chair and talk to him like I've never talked to him. I would've never sat in his chair then, when he was alive. I would've sat in the kitchen at the big maple table. Or on the couch. Look at that old couch—it looks dated; it looks dusty. Hank never liked pink, I knew that, but he never made a fuss about it. He would've been sitting here, in his chair. I couldn't have sat here. "Hank. I'm crushing you. This chair isn't big enough for two big bodies. I don't know what I am anymore. I thought I knew—for a while I knew—when I was in there, in the scene, I knew who to be... I feel like I know people, but I don't know anybody. I only knew you and I didn't know you. Hank. There was nothing to know. What were you, old man? What was I? What is anybody when they just roll it over, roll it over, what show, what dinner, what life? Hank!" I cry. Scream and cry. I heave and weep and scream and cry.

I stay in the chair, not knowing why I'm crying, not knowing why I should get up. I turn on the television. I guess I haven't turned it on in almost three months. I've watched TV, sure, in the kitchen, in the bathroom, from my bed— but not the big set from Hank's chair in the living room. I've done other things too. I've sat at the computer. I've listened to the radio. I've walked around. And sometimes, other times, I did none of those things. I sat on the porch. Those were nice nights until the darkness would take down the dusk and leave me cold. But on the porch when the sun would set, I could see out onto the street lit up in old yellow. All the way down Cedar to the intersection at Mill. It wasn't a busy intersection, but it felt like life was happening, and, until the sky swallowed it up, I liked those nights.

The TV powers up half a second after I hit the button. Like it's got its own ideas. The Sportsman Channel logo bug in the bottom left tells me that Hank was the last person to pick the channel, the last person to touch the remote. There's a commercial for a pro shop followed by Jerry Howe's jingle. It's silly; I always thought it was silly. But Hank thought pink couches were silly. He thought our pink bathroom was silly. I never told him I thought Jerry Howe's jingle was silly, and he never told me it wasn't. Little zip-zapping miniature Jerrys swish across the screen; laser pings and an up-tempo synthesizer beat out a thirty-second tune. *Jerry Howe's Fish 'n' Tips*. My chest tightens. I sit and watch Jerry Howe until I feel like I'm floating. Not because of Jerry, not Jerry, maybe because of Hank—Hank. My chest is tight, my heart beats in my throat, and my eyes, again, are hot, hot like my body under the sun when I lie in bed with the light streaming in through the curtains. My eyes are hot. I close them, listen to Jerry talk about lipless crankbait. Jerry Howe—he knows too much; he tells too much. He's always annoyed me with his authoritative drawl.

I open my eyes, ready to look disapprovingly into the sure face of Jerry, and yet the way he holds his fingers toward the camera after rigging a craw weedless—there's some softness in that. An old man whose fingers aren't what they once were. Knobby and stiff. An old man who now, after thirty years on the air, sometimes gets his cameraman to tie the knot. Which type of knot I wouldn't know—Palomar maybe. The knowing is useless to me, and now, now that his hands ache with arthritis, the knowing is useless to him. He can still tell it, but not with his fingers. His flat fingers. They're all one shape. Each finger a meaty rectangle bending stiff at the crease. Indelicate but kind.

***

This HIT is a test to determine cause. I answer. I don't ask.

SCENARIO: Matthew loved to ride his bike.

  LINK 1: Matthew's birthday was coming up.

  LINK 2: Matthew's funeral was coming up.

RESULT: Matthew's new bike was red.

SELECT ONE:

  LINK 1 IS MORE LIKELY TO HAVE CAUSED
  RESULT THAN LINK 2.

  LINK 2 IS MORE LIKELY TO HAVE CAUSED
  RESULT THAN LINK 1.

***

It's been three weeks since I turned off the Ujang Feeling file notifications. One too many fried fish sandwiches. Like I'm full and all I can do is hold my belly and roll around.

I get a notice in the mail to go down to the Stockton PD and sign some paperwork. I can't, or don't bother, making sense of the paper they've sent; the print is small and technical with my name pasted here and there. I don't read it carefully. I've been moving slowly all day. The notice says to appear the following week, and I consider perhaps it's a preamble to jury duty. In my entire life I've never received a notice for jury duty. Penny did. She told us she spent the whole day in a courthouse waiting for her turn to be asked a question, any question, and nothing happened. She waited for over seven hours, missed all her shows, and then was sent home. She was told over and over by various lowly looking officials that she should wait until her name was called. It was never called. Some names were called; some names were not. So maybe that's the thing they've sent the notice over.

The following week I walk unhurriedly to the PD. I stop at the ATM on the side of the Savery to pull cash in case I'm stuck sitting around somewhere waiting for my name to be called, and I'm tired and hungry, and all I want while I wait is a chocolate bar from the vending machine, but I don't have any change at all, I don't even have cash to turn into change.

Above the ATM screen, there's a small round mirror. I don't know if it's a camera or else meant to reflect myself to myself in case I start thinking up scams. A self-checking camera, me watching me. "Good one," Hank says.

No, Hank, okay. But it is strange, so I stop for a moment to watch my own eye, big and brown with burst veins on the lids and scraggly pointless remnants of eyelashes. An eye like my eye, but not—a reflection, a distortion. And when I stop looking, I no longer see, unless I keep it rolling, somehow keep it rolling, trade an eye for a greater eye, an extended eye. And like some mythological monster granted a mean fate, not to see death but something akin to it: infinity, eternity stretching before and behind, a screaming vibrating endless trill. Cowered then before the meaninglessness of endlessness, knowing that death, even if great, does not compare. "A fate worse than death," Vivienne LaRoque's faithful butler Dorian quips with his chipper British accent. He trades in clichés, but apt ones. I smile and, slower still, distracted by roaming eyes and a handful of cash, walk on.

It's a ways off, the PD, past the Farmer's, beyond the library; it must be three or four kilometres away. I walk, but it's a nice day, I gave myself lots of time, I don't mind moving slow. It's full spring, and things seem new, seem crisp. I'm here like an old tree ready to weather another season.

I spend three blocks behind an elderly couple—eighties, I'd guess, late eighties, early nineties—each with a cane. A paper-thin man on the left, against the traffic, cane in his left hand, his wife's arm through his own on the right. A skeletal woman on the right, against the dead grass, cane in her right hand, her husband's arm through her own on the left. They don't walk, they waver, they float, they sway toward the sun. I wonder if they're loving people. I wonder if they're trapped. I wonder if I lacked love. I wonder if I was able. Hank was right, wasn't he? I needed to be kept busy. Hank was right? To keep himself from me? *Accept it, somehow accept it.*

The couple goes west on Ingersoll. I pick up my pace. I run. I run for a minute, less than a minute; I run as long as I can run. It's not much of a run. It's a tossing of weight, a heaving. I'm throwing myself down the street; I'm panting; I'm gasping, and maybe my heart will burst and bleed and stain the ground, and the clash of the coral-coloured raincoat with my burst and bloody heart will blind their eyes when they walk on and over from whatever was waiting on Ingersoll. Twenty seconds of running, of heaving, of breathing, I get away. I escape. I expel something. A young voice calls out, "Crackhead!" and some kids laugh, but I don't look up. I keep my head down; I keep my heart beating.

My ankles ache by the time I get to the station. They seem swollen, and I sit in the waiting area. Not a vending machine in sight. I think about taking a taxi back, but then, I'm in no hurry. What if I walk back even slower than I've come? What if I rest along the way? If it takes me a week it won't matter.

After an hour in the waiting room, a man in a creased uniform peaks his head around a corner. He curls his finger to beckon me over. I scowl involuntarily and follow him into a cramped yellow office. It smells like a bedroom, personal, musty. Things seem old but not unclean. The pen he hands me looks beaten up, like it's been found and refound and, through it all, keeps writing.

"Miss or missus?" the old bald man asks.

"Miss, I guess—no, I don't know now—missus," I assert. "Mrs. Nimmo... No...Norma is all right."

"Well, Norma, I'm Officer Bowring and we've asked you to come down just to sign this little peace bond. There isn't much to it. Essentially in Section 810 of the Criminal Code, we have this little passage that describes a scenario in which a peace bond may—" Officer Bowring reads slowly, in a stilted manner, from a sheet on the desk flat in front of him "—'be laid before a justice or peace officer by or on behalf of any person who fears on reasonable grounds that another person will'—" Officer Bowring looks up at me, with a stupid little perfunctory smile "—in your case, commit an offence under Section 162.1, which—again we're talking about your case—refers to one 'who knowingly publishes, distributes, transmits, sells, makes available, or advertises an intimate rendering of a person knowing that the person depicted in the rendering did not give their consent to that conduct, or being reckless as to whether or not that person gave their consent—,"

"This isn't for me," I tell him, rising.

"How's that, Norma?" When he says my name this time, he sounds insolent. I hate him. I hate his scabby bald head, his dry old lips cracked in the middle, and the bored way in which his eyes drift over me.

"Oh, all I mean is that it isn't for me. I think you mean someone else."

"One Miss Marigold Rose has come down here; she's gone through the process, Norma—that's 67 Cedar Street? Oh, darn it, let's have some ID. I didn't ask for ID."

At the mention of Marigold's name, I shake. There's a stone in my throat; my eyes cross. I sit down and fumble through my foolish wicker purse, searching for my ID. Everything seems strange and overdetermined. My wedding ring is tight and brilliant and shivering on my hand, which is hunting for a floral print wallet inside an obscenely oversized impractical wicker purse filled with loose cash and local flyers.

The purse is from Mexico. Acapulco. Margery bought it for me when she visited about six years ago with Penny and Helena, a sweet old British lady with a teacup collection who Penny knew from the home. They stayed at an all-inclusive resort, drank margaritas (*Margie with her Marg!* Margerie had written of herself on the back of a photo), wore big silly beach hats, and kept their old skin covered. They invited us, but Hank hated the heat. He hated air travel altogether. "Too much bother," he'd said. And now, standing here undone, digging through a wicker purse I don't know why I picked out of the closet today, while brittle little strands of woven wicker snap and fall on a threadbare grey carpet, I have a deep pang of regret that I never went to Mexico with Margery, Penny, and funny Helena. Hank or no Hank, I wish I'd gone.

"Marigold?" I ask shakily, and hand Officer Bowring my ID.

"You know her then?" He has such an unassuming way of asking. It annoys me that he doesn't seem to believe or disbelieve anything I say. He takes it all as new information, just not very interesting information.

"I—I—I know her grandmother..."

"Ah, okay, here we are. Marigold's deposition claims that—let's see, where is it... Here... You don't know her grandmother. It seems, she thinks, you have information on her or about her and, well, this is why she's done up this peace bond. She thinks you're looking to distribute or otherwise gain from this information. She thinks—"

"Distribute? I don't... I mean, I don't have any information. I don't have, I don't know, I mean, not really."

"You know what, Norma, we don't even have to go into all that. We've got here some sworn testimony from a couple of folks down at the Savery—I guess you know the one, off Mill Street—and that's enough to get this peace bond signed, sealed, and delivered, you might say. I wanted you to come down here to give it a look over, give it a sign over, or if you refuse, well then, not a problem, but we'll have to set a court date, at which point you can go into it." Officer Bowring looks past me and makes a dismissive gesture to someone. I turn to look, but the other officer's already walking away; I can only see his back and a small stain of sweat growing out of a leather belt over a saggy pair of black pants. I look at Officer Bowring, but he makes no indication that anyone was standing there or that someone standing there was anything to think about or puzzle over.

"I didn't... I don't..." I say but feel like I could scream, faint, collapse on the floor. I feel my ankles throbbing. I try to pit the throbs of my ankles against the throbs of my heart. I close my eyes, breathe deeply—it's like a reflex, like being guided by a body that's finally decided it's on my side. "What do I have to do?" I say slowly, careful not to let my voice catch, not to let the catch be heard.

"Well, let's see..." he drawls.

I want to scream, *Don't you know! Don't you know anything! You small stupid little man, why don't you know!?* But I sit self-possessed, breathing, with my eyes loosely closed.

The fluorescent light from the small, windowless office is red against my eyelids. He continues after a pause punctuated with little "hmms" and little "huhs."

"We didn't use to do this part," he sighs, "but here we go," he says, triumphant but mild. "'The defendant agrees to keep the peace and be on good behaviour for no more than twelve months—' No more?" he quips. "Why no more?" He chuckles spastically. "'The defendant must stay away from the complainant's home and place of work. The defendant does not contact the complainant, their family members, or co-workers. The defendant does not distribute any information about the complainant, their family members, or co-workers…' And that looks to be it. Shouldn't be too hard, should it?" he finishes flatly, pushing the paperwork toward me. I sign quickly and make a strange little bow before asking to leave, accepting a nod, and racing away.

Through the waiting room, out the door, I'm at least three blocks from the station before my ankles ache and beg. I collapse on a bus-stop bench, breathing quickly. I might come undone, start gnashing my teeth, pulling my hair, shrieking. I can see myself in the street flailing and hollering, a deep unearthly bellow through my bowels, my intestine, travelling up, gathering speed. I reek, I retch, I bang my head against the pavement: *Nothing's wrong. Nothing's wrong.*

Sitting at the bus stop in near delirium, I'm outwardly still—no one would have any reason to see me.

Marigold must've given them the paper with my address. That's how they knew me. For a moment I feel betrayed by the girl, but, of course, shouldn't she feel betrayed? Betrayed by Amber Goodwin? By Inspector Mcreally? By Laeticia Matthers and the HopeHouse sham of paid and packaged empathy?

No one even asked me my connection to the whole event. No one cares about how I know what I know if I know anything at all. They see my fat body, loose dress, expanded orthopedics, wicker purse, and fuzz-top of a grey head and think, *Nothing. Nothing about this one.* And then they wave their hands dismissively. That must've been Mcreally standing behind me in Bowring's office. Bowring must have dismissed him, sent him back, said with a wave, *She's nothing. It's nothing. Harmless, this fat witch.*

Are they setting me up? Or maybe there's an incest/molestation department and a completely distinct stalked-by-an-old-woman department. Or maybe Marigold doesn't know that I really know anything. Maybe she couldn't think of anything incriminating to tell them. "She offered me tea," said the deceitful child. Maybe Doris defended me. And the meat-counter woman. The young man who did the interview. They know I'm nice; they know I'm good. Aren't I?

You know what? Maybe Bowring is just a bad cop. He's no good. Maybe he was supposed to ask, supposed to know, but he just pressed ahead, chuckled to himself, tried to close up the case. Nothing is playing properly. No one is doing the things they're supposed to do. They all have bad information and bad personalities, and they don't know how to make a story play, don't know how to make the audience stop screaming at the scene. Nothing is well-assembled, so I sit on the bench and I think about going back, revealing myself, revealing Bowring. Taking the whole lot of them down. But it seems like just another direction to be wrong in. There is no right. Or I'm not reading it right! There's only mess. Mess and television.

I sit on the cold wire bench for hours. Several buses pass. It's dusk; the sky is blue and black along the horizon. Officer

Bowring honks the horn of a ridiculous white Oldsmobile with rust gathering around the tire wells and dust obscuring the windows. "Norma!" he shouts plainly. I think of the Quickburger robot. "Norma!"

I walk or hobble over to the dirty white car. "What is it, officer?" I say dryly, as though I've never been less amused, as though the man is putting me out by calling me away from my perch at the bus stop.

"I'll give you a ride, Norma."

I get into the car without accepting. The interior is a plush burgundy that feels old and chalky.

"I seen you sitting there and I thought I'd offer you a ride," he says redundantly and without expression.

"So you did, officer. Thank you." I give him the address, and we're quiet for the rest of the ride.

"I'm not crazy," I tell him, getting out of the car.

"Well, whatever you are," he says plainly, looking into my eyes.

"Thank you," I say, and wobble inside.

***

HIT:

SCENARIO: Brenda loved to make people happy.

LINK 1: Brenda filled a bowl with human waste.

LINK 2: Brenda filled a bowl with bonbons.

RESULT: Everyone in the office was happy.

SELECT ONE:

LINK 1 IS MORE LIKELY TO HAVE CAUSED
RESULT THAN LINK 2.

LINK 2 IS MORE LIKELY TO HAVE CAUSED
RESULT THAN LINK 1.

***

Vivienne LaRoque had a recurring dream that Phillip was going to ask her to marry him. It was a gauzy Vaselined dream that flitted in and out of flowered corners—a white light shining down on Vivienne, the matriarch, the hero. Awoken by the screech of a tire or a peel of thunder, Vivienne would sit up in bed, rain beating the windowsill, with a look of resolution, but then, neither soft nor floral, Vivienne's dream became a delusion that only the viewer could see— the viewer and Vivienne's faithful slave Dorian, who acted as both henchman and conscience, giving Vivienne a soul against which to try herself.

But was she not justified? She was basically *married* to Phillip; he had essentially *promised* himself to her. Was Hera not justified? If the pathetic Semele knew not what she could look upon, a clever girl could keep her king. So Vivienne plotted but knew what was good and sacred—this love, this child she would give herself by the stolen seed of her drugged lover.

But alas, when the king falls ill, Vivienne is foiled—foiled but not defeated. Vivienne knew she could convince Phillip to commit absolutely—if only she were pregnant, if only she held the heir. The usurping nurse, however, the dainty delicate Juliana, wiping his forehead and whispering softly, was the kink Vivienne hadn't accounted for. And Phillip, now convinced of Vivienne's deceit, woos yet another stupid mortal lover. Oh gods! Oh Vivienne!

***

Norma Nimmo: I'm a sponge soaking up dirty water.

***

Wilma's on 10th is smaller than the Savery. Smaller than the Farmer's too. The aisles are close together, and there's an overall impression that everything on the shelves has always been there, and even when the goods were new, they were off-brand or failed exercises in product diversification: SpaghettiO squares, once-popular TV show characters replace the animal in the cracker. The fresh fruit and veg section seems tacked on, like they stuck a shelf between the bakery and the frozen foods and tried to force an aisle out of nothingness. Apples tumble frequently from the tilted, makeshift bin onto the dusty floor. Wilma's does, however, stock some surprising pre-made foods. Like I think they buy from local old ladies, buy their pies, their ham salads. A marvel of gelatin moulds and meat loaf sandwiches. Things that seem like children's nightmares are always in stock at Wilma's, so I guess everybody grows up to love Spam balls.

I walk toward Wilma's, past the Savery, not even looking, not allowed inside, not really, trying not to think about it, shaking it out of my head like maybe my mind works like an Etch A Sketch. It does a little. But it recurs, recurs, two ghostly hands turning the knobs. I walk on, walk and sometimes shake my head.

The day is lovely spring, and I like to walk like taking the dog out, like beating an old rug, spring-cleaned, touched by sun and air, making me feel my own skin—but only just, only lightly. If the wind were too heavy, if the sun were too hot, I'd turn back. I'm not up to it. I need what I'm getting from the bright light, from the unreal blue—I need them to be nice to me. But why, stupid old woman—*Don't*. But why should anyone, anything, be nice to you— *Stop*. What have you done, what have you ever really done for anybody— *Please*. You never believed in anything, did you? Shake. Whatever I am, I'm it.

Walking to Wilma's in the sun, letting maybe, when I can, the soft wind whoosh through my ears—it'll be better, it'll be better. Open the doors; open the windows. Sh. Sh. Sh. Sidelined then by signage on the Oneiroi Inn Hotel and Conference Centre:

POWER-U FEMALE ENTREPRENEUR CON

I take a detour. What am I thinking? I'm thinking: *Why not me?* I'm thinking: *If not now—then. Like before—less now— but maybe what I could've been. Or even like a pet kept in my pocket, a squirming worm squirming still.*

The conference room has tall ceilings and a long table along the wall covered with pastries, sandwiches, tea, and coffee. It's nicer than Hank's funeral spread. I hadn't meant to skimp; I guess I didn't know it could be this nice. Besides, who would've eaten it all? Maybe I should've called his old factory, made an announcement on the PA in the warehouse; maybe I should've drummed up enthusiasm for a really nice spread, not so much for a really nice man, but still *a man*, my man.

The conference room is cheery with oversized bundles of spring flowers and tropical imports. Pinks, lavenders, whites, and greens—dahlias, orchid twigs, magnolias, and amaranth, baby's breath, Bells of Ireland, and Peruvian lilies. It smells more like spring in here than out there. Maybe it's the circulating air, the concentrated spring. Maybe the spring flowers brought in from all over the world make reassembled spring concentrate seem like the real spring while the real spring withers and whines in mushy dead grass. I decide I want a pink dahlia. I want it selfishly and needlessly. It feels like the reason I've come. But it isn't the reason. What is? I'm a woman. I can be POWER-U or POWER-ME too, surely.

I fill my plate with almond pastries and little baklavas. I pour a mint tea and take a seat in the front row. I don't know if any of the women are looking. I just saw the spring flowers, smelled the spring flowers, felt small in a big room, and sat ready, ready for something to happen.

The other women settle in around me. It isn't a full house, so the seats on either side of me are empty, but there are pockets of well-dressed women in blue suits, red shoes, with smooth hair, funky glasses, women laughing and gripping each other's arms, women ready to be where they are, and when the host appears, they hoot. They shout, "Woot!" and "Go, Lexi!"

A blond woman in melting makeup and a cream-coloured power suit appears on the low stage. "Oh my God, I am *so* happy to be here. You have *no* idea. This is my *favourite* place. I am here *for* you, I am here *with* you, and let me tell you, we are going to get into it! Dig deep. So you all know me, I'm Lexi Kendrick, founder of POWER-U, author, entrepreneur, influencer, and, of course, mom—I never forget that—*that* is truly my most important job, my proudest accomplishment, but it doesn't define me, not exclusively. I, like so many of you, do it all. And I want to start by acknowledging that fact so it might help you to let yourself acknowledge *yourself* to yourself and really *own* your accomplishments. I want you all to give yourself *permission* to be proud of yourselves, to *value* yourselves, even to *brag* about yourselves. We're not talking humble-bragging here—brag big, girls! Pump yourselves up! Pump each other up! Brag, brag, brag about everything you are! And most of all, I want you—all of you—every last one of you—to give yourself permission to *breathe*. Let go. Be you. But I will say this, I will say this: if you have an agenda, you know, you're here, you're ready to mingle, you're ready to make connections—because that's what this is really about—just leave that agenda at the door, okay? Just sit back and let the magic happen. Okay? Okay. So who's ready? Who's ready? Let's start with a show of hands. How many of you feel almost *preordained* to do the work that you do?"

I put up my hand because everyone puts their hand up. But I'm getting nervous. I really don't know what she's talking about. Is this about business? Which business? What kind of business? Can you be preordained for business? Like magic? What magic? Is it visible magic? Tangible magic? I'm in over my head. These women are breathing deeply and readying themselves to be lifted up, to transcend, and I'm sure for an instant, for longer, I'm becoming increasingly sure they can smell the difference. "She isn't transcending!" one shouts, her knotless bowl cut shimmering like a brown satin dress she wears on her head, while the other women turn and scowl, their spirits brought down to earth for one ugly moment, Lexi Kendrick's voice growing deep and real, and then, with a low grumble, she commands her legions of lovely, wealthy, peace-seeking, magic-making POWER-Us to boo me or bite me or otherwise let me have it. I hop up, nipping the terror while responding to it, making my motions seem strange and forced, unnatural and awkward. Everyone looks—questioning faces, some incredulous, already doubting my value, my applicability: "I wonder what *she* does." "Yeah, *really.*"

"Excuse me," I say, and try to leave but trip on the empty chair next to mine and fall sideways into the row behind. It feels bad. I'm broken; I'm sure I'm broken. Women are hollering and twisting to get out from under me. They're upset, disgusted. I make my way to my feet; I offer my hand to the small blond woman with square teal glasses crushed beneath me, but she looks at me dirtily, and I'm afraid she's about to out me, reveal what I am, but it's already apparent; it's apparent in my posture, in my shallow breath, in my old-lady shoes.

I see security, an overweight teenager with a pussing face walking slow-motion toward me. There's no alarm, though it feels like an alarm is slowly sounding, like the women are all breathing together and exhaling one single siren cry, while I moan with a loud gravelling rasp that cuts through, upsetting the shrill collective. I hear Lexi on the microphone drawl, "Oh my *God*," as I dodge the security guard who saw me and my old face and my sack dress and didn't expect any kind of dodge, not even a slow careful one. I snatch a pink dahlia from a large bouquet and send the massive vase crashing to the floor. The soft wide hands take hold of my forearm and demand that I drop the flower.

"I'll go. I'll go," I say, trying to shimmy out of his grip, but his white meat-hands are too wide and they pinch my thinning skin. I let the long-stemmed flower fall, and I let him take me to the door.

All the while he's saying, "We don't need to call anyone, now, do we? We don't need to have anyone come pick you up, do we, lady?" in this idiotic way that betrays an air of haughty professionalism with barely bridled joy—joy!—to finally be useful—and before those POWER-U females, no less. This guy is having his day. I stay quiet, whimpering at times so he might pity me and loosen his grip and I can run back and grab the dahlia, but alas I give in, remembering that I at least filled my purse with tea bags.

And then that wasn't it. That wasn't the end. The end never came; I'm still in the middle. After an undignified ejection and the loss of the pink dahlia, I stand on the street in front of the Oneiroi Inn, strangely pleased with myself. Proud of what I've done as if I've done something. Stuck it to someone, to anyone who believes in anything. Where did you find your belief? Was it written in the sky? I let my thoughts run free through my rotting mind, and pictures swim and float and sink as is their whim, independent from me, my censorship, my shame, my guilt. I'm high. Reckless.

I see a too-tidy man strolling down the street, the far side of the street across from me. He's stiff, cross-eyed. He walks and wears a tight-fitting suit, blond hair plastered to his forehead by gel or sweat or both. He looks as though he's fled, has been fleeing, has come out on the other side of it, still menaced but no longer pursued. I scream, I shout, "Doug! Doug Deleanor!" He turns and looks but continues walking. "DOUGLAS!" I put my whole belly into it; I want him to see me. He turns again while walking, and I call one final time, "Doug!" This time he doesn't turn. And I move along, nearly forgetting what I've come out of the house for, on the precipice of self-disgust, creeping illness. I push it away. Resume the walk to Wilma's.

***

HIT: Determine the Truth of the Following Statement:

CONTEXT: A person wearing a robe and a pointed hat is holding a basket of bananas.

STATEMENT: All bananas are yellow.

IS THIS STATEMENT TRUE, FALSE, OR NEITHER?

What world is this? Is this a world where anything exists outside of the statement, outside of the scene? Does the wizard determine the truth of colour beyond the confines of his own basket? Can I imagine that by using the word banana there is a model banana upon which the word is suspended and the time between asking the question and answering the question has been short enough that bananas have not been cloned in orange or even pink? Do you want to know what I know or what I am deceived by having known? Can you tell me what colour banana you're planning for a future engineered by the bot insisting on this statement? No. You can't. No one can. An underlying order willed into being by an arbitrary identification of patterns, of pieces, of parts joined by keywords, by thoughts echoing the keyword and driving stilted movement—the movement of the body—the movement of my body—in answer to the imposed unorder of abstracted pattern recognition made obvious.

***

HIT:

SURVEY: Read the following paragraph and answer the question below:

Andrew has committed a crime. He's enjoyed a life of privilege and luxury. At the age of twenty-three, he was caught up in a Ponzi scheme and charged with two counts of fraud. His sentence is anywhere from eight months to eight years.

QUESTION:

How long should Andrew be imprisoned for?

*** *** ***

On my way into Wilma's, the automatic door shudders open, my eyes adjust to the low yellow lights, and I'm overwhelmed by the smell of a broken freezer, cold, old, and rotten. The Savery was renovated less than a year ago, and there's something—one might mention in a survey or on a questionnaire—refreshing about walking into a grocery store with high ceilings, diffused light, and the feeling that everything has almost grown there. A trick of the senses: "Which fruit seems more likely to have grown under the soft white lights and gentle mist of this newly renovated grocery store? This one? Or that one over there? In which store do you feel more clean? More lively? More connected to the world?"

Wilma's is dingy—covered in a coating of filth that can't be cleaned, that age presses into the cracks, the seams. *I don't belong here!* I cry to Dorian, powerfully, dramatically, with Daytime Emmy–getting passion. But he doesn't answer, because of course I do. I do belong here.

Wander the aisles, look for deals. It's busy, but unlike the Savery, everyone here feels old. The Savery is full of bustling mothers and well-dressed aunts. At Wilma's, a walker blocks aisle three, CANNED GOODS, and an oxygen tank blocks aisle four, TEA SYRUP BAKING. In the Savery, if you sneeze, it rings out over the PA system and a well-dressed man slides in with a tissue. At Wilma's, vibrating through the air, a perpetual cough, one long loud ineradicable hoarky rattle.

With my cart half-full, I make my way toward the till, feeling slow and tired, old and ugly, and also like *Okay, okay, stop wanting something else*.

The cashier looks like an old baby. She has pudgy cheeks that squish a small pointy nose into place, platinum blond hair tied up with ribbons into a senseless knot factory, and purple-shimmer shadow mopped over her heavy lids. I load my items onto the conveyor. The conveyor stops. The old baby stops. I look at her, my head to one side, sucking at the corner of my mouth. How long can this last? The belt's frozen. The old baby's frozen. I look around; nothing else is frozen. At least twenty seconds pass. I should say something, but I wonder how long it will go on. Motionless, her hands in a doll-like pose, one slightly higher than the other, looking at the screen in front of her. I wait another incredible twenty seconds, look around again, open my mouth to speak.

"My register froze," she says loudly without looking at me, but still beating me to speech, then resumes scanning.

I almost ask her about the malfunction, but think not, think that moments come and go, inexplicable things are said and done and consequences are endured and built upon; new things are introduced; unassimilated bugs branch out, live the defect, are unable to hold all the new consequences together and generate anything like integrity, while the inhabitants struggle to understand anything like the whole of it, relying instead on what we've made, and has made us, and what lies outside our collective organizing abilities, brought into being and gone beyond, to lead us. Inevitable dysfunction.

"It happens all the time," she says.

I try to answer politely, but my voice glitches. "A— O— Oh," I say, and smile, and leave.

∗∗∗

On my way out of Wilma's, it becomes clear that I've gathered too many groceries. I've got four plastic bags and they're heavy and the plastic is stretching thin at the handles, weighed down by cans of ravioli and day-old discount tourtière. Other things too, normal things: bird eggs, bovine breast milk. I know I have at least two pounds of orange cheese in one of the bags. I'll have to take the bus. I walk toward the stop, resigning myself to the stink and the dust and the hostile faces. Once again I sit heavily on the wire seat of the bus stop. And once again a dirty car pulls up and shouts my name. "Norma! Norma!" I walk toward what looks like a beat-up purple limo, odd and never elegant. A tinted window rolls down.

"Officer Bowring. I haven't done anything."

"No, Norma, no, I was just driving by. I saw you sitting here and I thought, well, isn't this funny?"

"You didn't know I was here? No one called you? You didn't follow me here?"

"No, Norma, I didn't." He laughs his little spastic chuckle in exaggerated disbelief.

"Funny," I concede dryly, unsure of my own intention.

"Well, let me offer you a ride once again. We'll make a tradition of it."

I'm relieved. I feel saved. My mind is starting to break up, running over the day. I want to be on my porch, in my kitchen, in my bathroom, dragging my feet along the familiar high-pile carpet of my bedroom.

The car is comfortable. Cushy, like his last one. The interior, this time, is mint green. Still rather stuffy with dust though, still rather sticky.

"This is a different car," I observe blandly.

Officer Bowring seems thrilled. "It's my father's car. He's ninety-six years old and he just bought this damn limo! Would you believe it?" His laugh aligns with the hum and chug of the car, which vibrate together in one deafening pitch for one soundless second.

"Hmpf," I say. "Your father is ninety-six?" I'm impressed. More impressed than I ought to be for something so common as not dying, and yet, much of my experience of life of late has been its end, so maybe I'm making sense. I feel something like emotion when I repeat back to Officer Bowring, "Ninety-six." The idea of age inspiring in me love like that which one has toward a puppy, or a little baby rabbit. Some tenderness wells up.

"He's ninety-six, he is. And crazy as ever." He laughs, this time nothing startling, nothing deafening, nothing upsetting to hear or feel vibrating through a body augmented by motors.

"So you're taking it out or what're you doing with it?"

"Takin' 'er out for a wash, see how she goes. He can't drive it; I think he just wanted to sit in it or look at it, but I'll clean it up for him. I thought it'd be nice, you know? I can take him for a ride around town now and again. Everyone always wonders who's in the back of a limo!"

I wonder if that's true. It seems true. It seems even like something that's been said before or thought before and so I can't think if I've ever wondered it or if only others have wondered it for me and maybe I think I've wondered it because I've heard that it's been wondered. Then I think of an old man wearing a knit cardigan and thick glasses grinning like a boy while being driven around in a big purple car. Again I feel something like a swell of emotion.

"That's nice," I say. My grocery bags are at my feet, and I feel free in the car. Like Officer Bowring and I go way back. Like he knows what I've done or what I've been or thought, and yet here I am in his father's car, feeling something nearly pleasant. No bus rage, no buzzing inner assault, no hucked shoes, canned vegetables, ravenous and toothy interjections, desperate bellowing erratic shapes flying toward a crouching wimpy narrator. Muted. It's nice to feel almost nothing. It reminds me of my life before madness, and I wonder almost to my own undoing (briefly, inconsequentially) if I can access any of my former selves.

"It's really a fun car to drive. People beep at me for no reason. Just because the car is long," he says innocently, and I nod gravely. His buzz travels along the length of the bench-style seat cushion.

I look around the car, seeing the fun in it, the strange silliness of an inconsequential wrecked and rusty thing— I dust the dash with my finger. I peer into the grey-caked ashtray. I open the glovebox and find a dead garter snake, stiff and dry. "Officer Bowring," I say, "there's a snake in the glovebox."

"Keep it," he says, and lets me off at my front door.

***

HIT:

SCENARIO: Daniel spends time in the garden.

LINK 1: Daniel has killed a cat.

LINK 2: Daniel has been eating worms for two days.

RESULT: Daniel thinks worms are a delicacy.

SELECT ONE:

LINK 1 IS MORE LIKELY TO HAVE CAUSED
RESULT THAN LINK 2.

LINK 2 IS MORE LIKELY TO HAVE CAUSED
RESULT THAN LINK 1.

***

First, I call him on the phone.

I pull out the phone book. Thin pages, small font. A book that seems old even when it's new, a book that smells like an artifact, a book that I keep and smell and use out of spite. All this information is available easier elsewhere. I can search-engine this; I can dial it up with my voice—saying into the ether, "Find Doug." And *it* will obey like he who obeys my request for a hot fish sandwich, for a cold pile of cream dipped quickly into chocolate, then air-cooled, creating a modern magic thing too small and stupid to be called magic. "Robo! Fetch me thy process. Amaze me, quick."

There are two Deleanors and only one D.R. I call the first and say, "Is this Doug?"

D.R. says, "It is." Casual and nice.

"Hi, Doug," I say. "You don't know me, but I wondered if you had time to discuss a few things. To sit down and have a little talk. I'm..." I struggle, having not thought anything out, having become, lately, but not lately, just always, just never noticed, unwilling to think ahead. "... Norma. Maybe your daughter has mentioned me." At the mention of Marigold maybe mentioning me, I feel my heart beat, feel my breath catch.

"Oh no," he says, chuckling, "are you another one of Mari's teachers?"

I lie. "Yes. That's right. When might be a good time to stop by?"

Stop by... he thinks (I can hear him think). I threw it out too early. I know it sounds strange, but it's been said, can't be unsaid. I can only wait with confidence. A pregnant kind of waiting where my will fills the wire. Anyway, he sounds simple, accepting. It might come off. I'm getting close to something I want but unclear on the shape and structure of the thing—like how would I get this thing into the house anyway? "Now or later, I don't care," he says, and I exhale, but he isn't listening, he's laughing again, "I don't really go out these days." His chuckles are incessant and infectious and sound real and rich. He has a nice laugh.

I walk, of course; I can't remember the last time I took Hank's car. I'm lying. I remember. Why do I lie? I lie because I like lying, because sometimes it sounds better to say a word than not say it, and the meaning of it is indifferent to the sound of it. I remember the last time I took Hank's stupid goddamn Chevy Spark out—a car that's so good on gas it annoyed me whenever we filled up the tank. "What're you smiling for?" I'd ask him sourly. Why couldn't I just let him have it? Just let him be happy, even if it wasn't a kind of happiness

I was used to seeing on him, a kind of happiness I thought looked good on him. A giddiness, a cuteness.

Maybe I hated it because that little aqua-coloured car brought him more joy than I did. Was I jealous of a car? I wasn't. Surely I could've pleased him if I tried. Surely I could've earned a satisfied smile. But instead I'd stomp around, arms crossed, pretending like I hated the feeling of being, like I'd never liked it, and like Hank hated it with me, and the only thing that kept us together was our smirks, our sneers, our long loud eyerolls. None of it was true. And yet, I'd have to do it again. Bring him back, raise him up, sit him in front of me, and when he turns up the volume on the TV, and when he dances his way back to the car from the pump, I cross my arms. I feel them cross just thinking about it.

Oh, but they loosen when I remember the dusty smell of him rising up in the car the day I drove to his funeral. Alone. I was sitting in his place, driving his car, going to see him off. And all I could think was *I hope it runs out of gas*. Well, so, push it down, once again. On this day, I leave the car.

I walk and find it not far but through an area in which I rarely travel. Doug lives in an apartment downtown. It's evening and people are about. Bustling almost. It's a mid-size town, but the bustle makes it feel big. Now distracted by thoughts of an aqua-coloured car, and every off-shift man in a coverall makes me close my eyes so I might not gnash my teeth right into him. I'm sorry for what I am. I'm desperate. I'm sorry.

"As I mentioned on the phone, Doug, I'm Norma."

"One of Mari's teachers, right?"

"Is she still in high school?" It's a strange question from a would-be teacher, but one that falls out of my mouth nonetheless as I stand at his door looking into his handsome, square-jawed face. I can't believe how good-looking he is. I pictured something really slimy, really sallow, like the gelled man on the street who fled from my shouting. But Doug is tanned, with creases around his eyes and an anachronistic drooping moustache that makes a cowboy out of him. He's of medium height, and the muscles of his arms gleam bronze beneath a thin white T-shirt. He looks so easy, half-smiling, twinkling, a man unable to be either truly surprised or dismissively complacent. A perpetual slow satisfaction creeps across the doormat.

"Now, shouldn't you know that?" he asks with a conspiratorial look.

You can tell a villain anything. "Oh, okay," I say. "Okay. I really don't know why I'm here. What it is, what happened is, I just type out files. I just find files from all over—they come from everywhere; they're on everything. They reach into everybody's lives, and no one seems to mind that they're dividing themselves up. I write them out. I don't add anything, just write them as I hear them and sell them back to the speaker, or sometimes, like with yours, I sell them back to the organization, to the official. And really, it's a strange thing to give yourself to the official and have the official think they can just trust whatever org they dig up, they find, any sitting-around anybody with nothing better to do than type out your life and think and think and think about you. But they do it; they all do it. What I'm really trying to say is that I'm breaking my NDA."

"Uh-oh," he says. "You're doing something you aren't supposed to do." He shakes his finger like I'm naughty, like we're naughty together. He pauses for a second as if considering what the real thing to do is, what it should be. I watch him.

But this might be a man who's never said no to anything.

He invites me in. I sit on a 1970s short-backed beige sectional and wait for him to bring me a can of beer from the kitchen. His apartment is minimal but not terrible. He's hung some pictures. He has a big TV on the wall opposite the couch with a classic rock channel playing over a black screen. He has a green rug under a glass coffee table, the latter of which is strewn with weed crumbs and rolling papers. I run over everything and return to the pictures.

There's a dated family photo with a dirty-blond woman in a blue blouse standing next to a clean-cut fellow in a plaid shirt. A little girl stands between them. I'd expected something different from Mona, something more crass, angular, abstracted. She appears, in this image, proud of herself, of her family, of the matching backdrop, and the can of hairspray in her hair. Her smile is wide and white-toothed. Marigold has apparently always been beautiful. She was a cherubic baby, an angelic toddler, and the girl suffered no awkward adolescence. Her school pictures alongside each other on the wall are a genealogy of disaffection. She has ringlets. She has freckles. She has, in her latest photo, weary defiance.

Doug pushes a beer into my hand, and his large fingers brush my wrist like sun-warmed driftwood, like the hands of a workingman, and for just a second I feel sad that the vision is incomplete, that it couldn't be what it should be because there is no should—only what we get away with. I sit on one side of the L-shaped sectional; he sits on the other. He cocks his head quizzically. There's nothing to do but ramble and hope.

"I learned about your family. That's what I can tell you. I learned that I was nearby. Nearby you and Marigold and your wife and your mother. I'm nearby Laeticia Matthers from HopeHouse, and Amber Goodwin, and even the ever-silent Inspector Mcreally. I'm nearby. I have access to you. Whenever I want. Whenever I want. Whenever I want." I say all this to him like I'm unravelling something. I'm panicked but sincere. *Norma's an honest sort*, he might think.

He nods and furrows his brow as though thinking through what he's supposed to feel and what he's supposed to say. A long pause. He could call the police, but he won't. He could shout and shame me. He could act indignantly and throw me out. But Doug leans back on the couch and looks at me with a low brow and a slow smile. He crosses one leg over his knee and sighs. He decides to tell me something.

"Minimum five years, that's what I'm looking at."

There's a silence, but it's his—I won't fill it.

"I'm lucky they let me out on bail. I would've thought I'd be a flight risk." He laughs. "I could live a long life on a beach somewhere." He laughs again. Another silence. "I'm hooped!" he shouts.

"When's the trial?" I ask him because he wants to be asked.

"A few weeks. I've done time before—weed, B&E when I was a kid, but nothing like this. Never anything like this." He shakes his head, and the sun through a high window over his left shoulder shines bright on his brown hair. He should be riding horses and sleeping by a fire. He should be staring at the ocean from the side of a yacht.

He tells me with an ease he can't shake, even when it clashes with his head, his heart, that he doesn't know how he'll manage. Sometimes, when he speaks, he looks up at me and I wonder if the look in his eye is remorse or fear, but I really can't say. It's as likely one as the other. It's as likely neither.

"Which beach?" I ask, and he laughs a yelping incredulous laugh.

"Who knows. Cancún? Are we gonna run away together, Norma?"

I laugh a queasy sort of laugh and drink my beer. I go through three beers talking to Douglas Rhodes Deleanor like one famous person to another, like we're being recorded and seen and known. Like something important is happening to us. I'm red in the face from excitement, from the thrill of saying things like, "Uh-huh [affirmative]" and "Okay."

But we're nothing to each other, and there's no way out of this. Doesn't matter what he looks like. It doesn't matter how he seems. It settles around us like a slow crash. Everything stops being funny. My fourth beer is empty. There's a silence, a sadness, and then, an awkward confession—like it's my turn, like I'm going to make myself take my turn.

"I'm worried that I don't feel the way I should feel...about Hank, my husband." In all my talk up until this point, I hadn't mentioned Hank's death. And to speak of him now, to this stranger—Doug Deleanor, incestuous molester, a man Hank would have abhorred on principle alone—to talk to him as though Hank were still alive is like living a dream. I get to go back and fix something, or pretend it can be fixed, or pretend I know what a fix would look like. Just for a second, talking to a face that feigns caring, or somehow really cares, I pretend.

"You don't love him anymore?" Doug asks with eyebrows high, face open.

"All I know is that we never have a kind word for each other. And that there's no problem. All our problems were settled forty years ago. The roots of our habits established.

This is just the shape of the tree." I look down and around at my wide body on the beige couch.

"It's never easy," Doug says, with a sympathetic squint of his left eye.

This odd intimacy established, his unsatisfactory comment issued, I need to say it now, I need to ask him now—to say what? to ask what?—*Did you, do you, love Marigold?* Can't ask, won't. I can answer it myself anyway. Maybe he loves himself more. Maybe he mistook love. Maybe she mistook love. Maybe, who cares, it's done.

In silence, we both consider the unasked question.

"I'd feel guilty, and then—" he shakes his head. "It's all over. Nothing else matters. There are times when I would do anything. When I will do anything."

So that's it. It's just the fact of the feeling, the feeling in the moment that makes acting on the feeling as good as good to him. Most people think they're good; they justify their behaviour or, at least, they don't think about it but settle it emotionally. The thing they need to be true becomes true because the feeling seems real, seems pure, because it hits as if sent from somewhere else. And whatever makes anyone corrupt isn't accessible, but something has to take the blame. Though Doug doesn't try to blame anyone or anything—not his past, his genes, not some social corruption. Maybe it's because I don't ask, and maybe I don't ask because I know it wouldn't be real if he had to make a story about it. We just talk like two famous people. But still, when he speaks, I know I'm looking for the defect, the thing that falls flat with words—trying to uncover something: "Oh, okay, I get it"— the giveaway. But he's illegible, or it's buried deep. Maybe it would take a lifetime to uncover. Maybe Mona sees it, maybe Marigold, maybe Rosa, but I can't find it, and it feels worse not to find it than to know it, because it messes with sense, it messes with meaning—to have him seem honest and likeable with his breezy half-smile, to see him as someone who sighs with humility, someone who has real beauty.

"I don't know why, but I'm glad you came by, Norma," he says, shaking his head with ease, like it's written for him.

"Doug." I say it like Hank would say it, strong and firm, like I know who I am, who I've always been—I put out my hand.

He shakes it, hard and dry, making me an accomplice in his false goodness, in his clean calm—and I freeze, like an old baby at a grocery store, for a second, under a second, fixed on the thick spittle of his lower lip. Normal human spittle though, isn't it? I wonder without words, with words that come later, about this slick and haunting spittle, a wet patch that could or would catch light in my mind forever after, so that when I think of Doug, if I ever think of Doug, it isn't of a kindliness he ought not to possess, a kindliness I feel obliged to deny him—it's of spit. Spit I willed into being. But he licks his lips, wipes his mouth, and gives out nothing else.

I walk home, and the work rush is done, but there are young people in nice pants headed to bars and restaurants. People who don't see me or need to see me. It's okay; I don't need anything from them. A mother says to her teenage daughter as though making a shocking confession, while the girl looks stiffly on, "I wanna buy a Subaru." A man with a mushroom cut shouts over his shoulder to a small crowd of tall women shivering in summer dresses, "Story of my life, eh?" An independent-looking toddler pedals a rusty blue tricycle quickly past. A casino suffering renovation with billowing white material partially obscuring its scaffolding flashes bright lights—the demanding signage without an obedient people below suggests something unreal, as though the singular sucking purpose persists in any condition—a ghost ship sailing the empty ocean, the dead fish sea. A woman wearing heavy plastic jewellery weeps flamboyantly and runs across the street after waiting for the walk light to signal. And two blocks from my house, a pair of disembodied pigeon wings lie on the sidewalk as though placed before me, bloody bones where the body should be.

***

Terrence Fenamore: I want to thank everyone who was able to join us on this call today. It's a banner day for the Copywriters of Canada Org. We have with us today Janice Highsmith, who's recently put out a very successful package for SoulHealth Botanicals-

Jeremy Weedler: Weed Your Way to the Garden of Eden, incredible piece of copy.

Janice Highsmith: Thank you, thank you so much, Jeremy.

Terrence Fenamore: Janice has a long list of accomplishments. She's put out copy for NewNog, BrainStam, Pie in the Sky, and Bushelmore. She spent seven years as the executive director of Xeoxi's and single-handedly brought Dr. Dan to the attention of the world through an unrivalled aromatic campaign. Janice, welcome, and thank you for coming here today. I know you're incredibly busy with your seminars, and I saw that your online girls group is growing.

Janice Highsmith: That's right, thank you, and yes, seeing a lot of gains in the copywriting for girls group, WriteHeartCopy. Thanks for coming to the call, everyone.

Terrence Fenamore: All right, okay, Janice. Well, I think what everyone is here to find out is basically one thing: how do you write successful copy?

Janice Highsmith: Well, let's see, I've been writing copy for SoulHealth and the alt-health community for many years, many, many years, and really, I think we all know the steps involved, am I right? Research! Establish credibility! Be compelling! We all know this from the major figures in copywriting, right? Gurus like Gene Benson and Darren Fosey. And let me tell you, if you haven't read copy by Fosey, get it. It is phenomenal.

Jeremy Weedler: Let me just interrupt there for a minute, Janice, if I may.

Janice Highsmith: Please do, Jeremy.

Jeremy Weedler:	Fosey's piece, *Free Bananas and Other Industry Secrets*, changed my life. Changed it. If you haven't read this copy, I'm telling you now, you need it on your shelves.
Janice Highsmith:	Absolutely. I know I have that one around here somewhere. Uh-oh! Maybe someone stole it!
Terrence Fenamore:	I buy it whenever I see it... This was released as a bookalog in '94 and you can still find it circulating... I buy it whenever I see it. I know I've had a few copies stolen over the years. I give it out as gifts to aspiring copywriters; you really can't have too many.
Janice Highsmith:	And Fosey does something in that package that I try to do with all of my packages: tell them, teach them, reveal the hidden cause, and then reveal the solution. I'm educating the prospect. We're teachers, you know? We really are. We educate the prospect to what the deficiency is and... Now, they may have heard of it, whatever it is, but they don't know that it affects them, it affects them every day... We educate them to their own deficiencies... We really... We make the unfamiliar familiar.

Terrence Fenamore: Great, great. That's really good. And, Janice, what, for this package, did you do differently? Did you invent... well, I know you can't just invent a new copywriting principle, but was there any technique that you followed or improved on, or was it just the old standards?

Janice Highsmith: As I've said, I've been doing this a long time. I came up in the direct mail circuit, and I know the ropes. It's just this, the hidden cause. You reveal the hidden cause, that thing that everyone has, everyone experiences, and you reveal the hidden cure. You paint a picture, that's what you do. A vivid picture that helps the prospect see themselves in your copy. They have to...they really have to feel like you're speaking to them. That's another thing: make it personal, speak on their level. Don't speak down to them. You'll lose your prospects that way. You're their best friend, they're your best friend. You want what's best.

Terrence Fenamore: That's great. That's really great. And, Janice, can I ask, is there a chance that if you bring in some of the more technical terms too early on in the package you'll lose your prospect?

They'll just go search it on their own? This question comes up a lot.

Janice Highsmith: That's the question these days, isn't it? Now that everything's available. Well, let me tell you, I have a couple of solutions to this problem. The first is simple: state everything upfront. Tell them everything you know. Be the research, introduce your credibles, your doctors, your experts, your blah blah blah. The second is this: transubstantiate. The word is the body is what you need it to be. Introduce the term, the phrase, the idea...a simple one perhaps...as something else, and have them read to transform the meaning, to make it theirs, to incorporate it into themselves. If you're talking about living until 150, we're not giving out that formula for free, we're not giving out the formula at all. We're alluding to it, we're suggesting it through results, and when the time comes, we drop the brand, we drop the cure... The price is no longer an issue because you've already sold the word. Understand? Is that clear? Make them believers. Now the word could come as magalog, bookalog, VSL, direct mail... You name it, you make them know it by making them know what they aren't, by making them see themselves in your creation.

Terrence Fenamore: Great, Janice, great.

***

SURVEY: Read the following paragraph and answer the question that follows:

Jordan has committed a crime. He's suffered a life of misery and deprivation. At the age of twenty-three, he robbed a gas station with a Bowie knife. He screamed, "Empty the register or I'll kill my dog!" to the terrified cashier at the counter. The cashier said quietly, "Please, no," and Jordan dropped the dog and turned the knife on the cashier. The cashier cowered, and Jordan made off with $150. The dog ran out of the convenience store and was hit by a car. The dog died. Jordan's sentence is anywhere from eight months to eight years.

QUESTION: How long should Jordan be imprisoned for?

***

I watch TV, but I don't watch TV. It plays in the background or risks becoming a farce of the current and embroiling me in all of it. Whatever's present, whatever's alive, when you redirect it toward this flat parody and let yourself loose on it, order is reconstituted.

To watch someone watch TV is to embarrass them unbeknownst to them. To walk past their window and see the screen on the wall, in the corner, colouring their house and crowding their life, is to watch a life already lived and lived elsewhere, repeated to little enjoyment, or too much enjoyment. It's strange. It's disappointing. And I can't endure it except to have it on in the background as an old friend who requires nothing but would balk at too attentive an inquiry, who would become tired if I pressed them but is happy to prattle on while they do the dishes—or while I do.

But sometimes, when I have occupied myself, when I have done various tasks, when I have helped those who need their soaps transcribed, when I have answered the questions that obsess these scammers, these academics, these marketeers, when I've taken my body around the block—I sit and think, *Now what?* I don't want to think it, but I think it. And having done everything else, I turn on the television as though to watch it rather than have it just bleating day in and day out, unnoticed like an old red-eyed goat; I maintain that I will pet *la bête*, and, more cat than goat, it turns, uninterested in my affection, and in turn I turn, also uninterested in my affection. Each image appears not as an image but as every other image, a mass of obsequious beauties, after me, just frothing. Each one attempts its own new, and its own new only furthers the old, but like a star with aching edges reaching slowly outward, outward. It's like it always was, like we always expected it to be, but now it's this pose, now it's that colour, it's hamming, it's fisting, it's mugging, and I'm bored beyond boredom before I let myself go and let the voice, body, disembody, have at it, just let them in.

I resist this, the initial disgust, until I look around and remember that I've done everything. That I live not by my own efforts but by default, and I see that I must watch TV or else decide now how to become somebody else, how to start over and every day after that become more of the new self. Say, "Today is the first day of the rest of my life," with outdoor lighting and the pursuit of life on the small screen, the big screen, wisdom shaped like wisdom but existing only in pockets—pursue practicalities and niceties, learn French, or else to bowl. In a world! Of possibility! You have no reason to get down! In a world! Of possibility! You have no reason to complain! And oh, I know.

Sometimes I find myself searching for other selves who, like me, feel, only for an instant, aimless, and then, after that, angry at everyone who would express their impression of aimlessness, and I search myself on search engines, like "sad old woman," or like "wandering widow," or like "feel no good," or like "point," or like "why," and find forums, places, zones of me's like me, other me's, and then these folks who feel what I feel but worse and always, or feel what I feel but rarely and less so, and I read their descriptions, which I understand as though I'd beat them out of my own brain, and I think now, now that I see that they've taken the time to give word to feeling, that they are quite dumb. "It's only a feeling!" I shout about them when I read about them. And like watching depravity worse than my own make itself a spectacle, I feel good, superior, and fine. That too fades into just another way to feel.

***

Christie Callister: But why? Why would frame your own brothers?

Thomas Kinder: Why? Why, she asks. Little Miss Perfect Christie Callister who's always had everything handed to her on a silver platter asks why. Listen here,

Little Miss Perfect, you couldn't begin to understand me. So just shut up or I'll shut you up.

Christie Callister: You can keep me down here for a day, a week, a month, but you won't get away with this. You'll never get away with this. My parents, my brother, they won't stop until they find me. You'll rot for this. Are you listening to me! You'll rot!

Thomas Kinder: That ought to keep you quiet for a while. When she wakes up, she won't remember anything from the past three days. But if everything goes according to plan, she'll still remember this face, our face—eh, brother?

***

Amelia Landover: Dorian, I want to see my mother. I mean Vivienne. Take me to her. Now.

Dorian: I would, miss, but Vivienne, she...she can't see anyone.

Amelia Landover: I understand if she doesn't want to see me after the way I behaved, but, Dorian, try to understand! My whole life was rearranged. I needed time to forgive her. But I thought we were past all that, Dorian! I...I need her. Please, Dorian, take me to Vivienne.

Dorian: I can't. You see, Vivienne...she's dead.

Amelia Landover: She's...*what?*

Don't worry about Vivienne. Don't anyone worry about Vivienne. Even when she walks into the sea, she comes out rolling, riding the waves, ready to fight for love like love means something.

Oh, why do I say what I say? I say don't listen to me. Can I help what I think? Can I help what I feel? What I am? Maybe. Maybe I just need the right show. I'll try, I'll try, I'll try to watch the right thing. I mean, what I meant to say was that I'll try to make the right friends—I meant, actually, I'll try to believe what I'm supposed to believe. And after a while I'll forget that I don't believe it.

You idiot, you old baby, it's not like it's easy for anyone, any human; HUMAN INTELLIGENCE TASKS have been beneficial to mankind, *obviously*. We can see more about us, what we are, what we could be, what we make ourselves into: feeding data, sifting data leading toward thinking/seeing/knowing, until the synchronous becomes the singular becomes the conscious unconscious whole—and what does that look like? Like one swollen drop, like one collective breath, before spitting, scattering exhalation—and the frenzy builds back up—and what does that look like? Like my labour, like my value:

HIT: Determine the Truth of the Following Statement:

CONTEXT: Several people are picketing the ocean.

STATEMENT: Some people are doing something.

IS THIS STATEMENT TRUE, FALSE, OR NEITHER?

***

"Hi-ho, Norma, I was hoping you could come down to the police station today. Just a little thing, no big deal." His voice is high and clanging over the phone.

"Officer Bowring?" My heart beats quickly. Like everything has been decided, though I don't know what. I don't know how to know what; I should've read the peace bond more carefully. Where is it? Don't I have a copy? I should've asked Bowring questions. I should've gotten a lawyer. But then, would I have had to lie to the lawyer? Would he have cared that I broke one or two measly little online NDAs? What did it matter? I signed them online, like agreeing to anything else I agree to, because it's the next step in the process. "What's this about?"

"It's nothing, Norma. Actually, I meant for you to sign three copies here, and you've gone and signed just one. It's my fault, my fault. Don't worry. But still, if you could come down and sign the other two, if you could do that, I'd... Well, I'm asking if you could do that."

"Sure."

I feel like I can trust him, like there's something about this old man and his old cars—they aren't nice old cars like the kind anybody really collects, or if they were becoming what people collect—because maybe there's a club for collecting anything like maybe there's a club for believing anything like maybe there's a club for listening to, loving on, dancing to, holding hands with, singing along to anything—these cars aren't well-maintained. He's just an old man with a few rusty cars, wearing transition lenses, showing up places in flowery shirts to drive me home. I don't know what he's about, but I feel like it isn't a set-up, like no one's going to be there ready to tackle me or trap me or trick me into something. Maybe that's it. That's maybe it, and so I walk the long walk to the police station and I get there and sit down heavily in Officer Bowring's musty office.

"Why do you walk everywhere, Norma? I seen that little car in your driveway."

"I like to walk. Or, anyway, I don't like to drive."

"Fair," he says disposably, and hands me the paperwork, which I sign and take my copy and review, or begin to review, what it is I'm signing but become bogged down by the language and just agree with myself, promise myself, that I'll be better, that I'll clean my house and everything else.

Officer Bowring says that he's off work soon and that he can, of course, drive me home if I'll just wait for him. So I sit in a waiting room that has no magazines and no music and no vending machine and feel uncomfortable and long to be outdoors, just anywhere else. A redheaded woman walks by in her police outfit, and I know it's her. It's Amber Goodwin. I don't need to look at her name tag, nor do I want to. It could be her. It might as well could be.

Bowring comes out in his civilian clothes, and it seems strange that he'd have me wait for him to put on little green shorts and pull up tall white socks. I wonder if he sits when he pulls up the socks or if he balances precariously on one foot. He walks stiffly, and I decide that he must sit to pull up his socks.

"It's like tradition," he says, "me driving you home."

"You said that," I reflect. "You said that last time."

"I may have," he concedes.

He stops the Oldsmobile in front of my driveway, and

we look at the house together. Two storeys high, white, built in 1914, and renovated sporadically over the years so that the different whites on the wood, the stucco, and the frames around the windows don't really match. It's been maintained piecemeal. The lawn, as well—half-weeded one week, over-mowed the next. One year, I planted perennials, the next year pumpkins—neither flourished. Officer Bowring stands before the house like a tree root protruding from the sidewalk.

"I'll offer you a drink then," I say, and he follows me to the porch, stopping to observe a large pile of newspapers on the right side of the door. "My husband had a subscription. I should cancel it."

"A good enough place for 'em."

He doesn't ask about my husband or his subscription. I'm glad of it. I look at Bowring's face. Open and bland. Clean-shaven, dry skin. A network of fractured pink veins spreads from the inside of his nostrils, along his cheeks, and toward his ears. His eyes are small and muddy. I can't tell what colour. Blue, grey, green, some variation. His eyebrows fan out like they're fighting the wind. He reminds me of an inflatable-clown punching bag. Always coming up smiling. Immune to basic violence. Amusing, upsetting, ridiculous.

He sits on the wicker couch on the porch, and a small puff of dust from the old pillow fills up the sun streams. "I like this house," he says, like he's getting ready to buy it.

I unlock the door, and the screen clatters behind me. I get two bottles of beer. "Beer okay?" I ask.

"Sure," he says.

"Or do you want tea?" I offer.

"Whatever you're having," he says.

"Or food or anything else?" I ask.

"Whatever you're having," he says.

"You got no preferences?" I ask.

"Whatever you're having," he says.

"You said that," I say. "You already said that."

"I may have," he says.

"And what if I told you I was going to have a cup of toilet water, Officer Bowring, what would you say then?"

"Sounds unwholesome, Nora."

"Norma. You know very well my name is Norma."

"Can I call you Nora though? It's easy to say. Nora. You don't even have to close your mouth to say it."

I let out an involuntary guffaw, and mouth the word *Nora*. "Sure thing. You got a first name, Officer Bowring?"

"Yep," he says absently, and looks down the street toward the evening sun.

I grunt, then giggle, strangely, giddily. "Well, what is it?

"Archie."

"Fucking Archie." I laugh and laugh and don't mind if he thinks I'm crazy, I laugh like I haven't laughed since I was a kid. I think while laughing that I can't remember laughing and snorting so loudly, so stupidly, in a hundred years. "It's been—" I puff to get my words out "—a hundred years."

He laughs too, his short spastic laugh, a little machine gun of hyphenated breaths. The sun seems stuck in the air, like an orange already peeled and left, skinless but whole, to hang. The sky twinkles in pink, and I think about how nice it is, how much I like it, how there aren't words that make liking it useful and there isn't anything to do with how much I want something from this feeling of liking and loving and wanting. My heart is pressing up against it, the slinky pink sky, and hurting, just holding itself in place with the bones in my chest, aching to get out.

"So you're a cop," I say, either trying for conversation or indulging a curiosity. "How come?"

"I thought I could be useful," he tells me plainly. "I dunno if I was." He sucks his beer and asks for another one. I hobble inside, ankles sore from my ceaseless parades.

"Sometimes probably," I tell him when I return, and hand him another beer. "Did you ever want to be something different?"

"Like a hunter maybe. Is that a job? I don't know. I don't think too much about what isn't."

"Like that song, you know, 'Can't always get what you want.' Like that, but 'you can't always *want* what you *get*'— like that, you know?" I shouldn't expect to make sense, to keep any sort of hold, no matter how tenuous.

"I guess like that," he says generously, "but I don't know the song."

"You know, like—" I sing "—Can't always get what you wa-ant, but try...and find...you got what you ne-ed!" It feels okay to be stupid and sing badly here with Archie.

He laughs and shakes his head. "I don't listen to music," he says.

"I just mean like the song they play on the radio. I don't mean you went to the concert or anything."

"I don't listen to the radio if I can help it. And I can't think of the song, but I try not to hear them anyhow." We sit quiet for a while. Then he says, as though he's been trying to form a thought or trying to word a thought that hadn't previously had anything like words to it, "I don't want that stuff messing with my mind, pushing me around."

"Like, 'Oh, this is what's real,'" I say, and surprise myself.

He goes on like he doesn't hear me, like he's finding words and he's going to believe in them for the moment, if only for the moment that they come out of his mouth. "Maybe if there was just one thing and not all these little things trying to cut through, unable to cut through, but pushing, pushing outward. Maybe eventually when everything turns inward…like, if there was just one piece of music, maybe I could listen to it," he says, looking perplexed but finished, satisfied, or content to be dissatisfied.

"Are you waiting for the second coming, Archie?" I ask him.

He snorts obscenely. "Whatever it is," he says oafishly. Then, in a breath of a voice: "Maybe we're reaching one— the middle of infinity."

"Sounds like another piece of music," I say, "coming out of your mouth."

"That's what I can't help, I guess," he tells me, and scrunches up his nose oddly in a way that mismatches the tone and timbre of his voice.

I learn that Archie likes the sound of birds and the sound of the train. I ask Archie if he can determine the difference between the sounds of the birds and the sounds of the train, and he laughs stupidly. I ask him if he can determine the difference between the sounds of a man singing and the sounds of a bird calling while a train drives by and the wind howls, and he laughs harder and harder and more desperately. I laugh too, and listen to the nearby birds and the far-off train until all the noises and Archie's voice are drowned by the sound of a street cleaner.

ACKNOWLEDGEMENTS

The author is indebted to Steven Mintzberg, Paul Carlucci, Melanie Simoes Santos, Norm Nehmetallah, Megan Fildes, the U of R English Department, Canada Council for the Arts, friends and penpals, and the world wide web.

Sarah Mintz is a graduate of the English MA program at the University of Regina. Her work has been published with Book*Hug Press, JackPine Press, *Apocalypse Confidential, The Sea & Cedar Literary Magazine,* and *Agnes and True.* Her flash fiction collection *handwringers* was published with Radiant Press.